COWBOY UP

AN ANTHOLOGY TO BENEFIT THE JUSTIN COWBOY CRISIS FUND

Edited by Carol Hightshoe

WolfSinger Publications ⸸ Brackettville, TX

DEDICATION

This book is dedicated to the rodeo cowboys, cowgirls, clowns, and all those whose grit, determination, and unwavering spirit keep the tradition of rodeo alive.

It is also dedicated to the memory of the horses lost at the Beutler & Son Rodeo Company in August 2024.

At every rodeo, where the dust rises and the crowd roars, the spirit of these horses will forever live on.

Editor's Note

I just want to say thank you to all the fans, contestants, secretaries, stock contractors, and other rodeo people I worked with during my time at the PBR as part of the fan club and at the PRCA as an operator (19) and a keyer (54). I loved talking to all of you, helping you with your rodeo entries and rodeos—it was a pleasure, and my wish is that you are all able to continue in this sport you love for as long as you desire.

TABLE OF CONTENTS

ABOUT THE JUSTIN COWBOY CRISIS FUND

Rodeo is a sport steeped in tradition and heritage, but it's also one of the most dangerous professional sports in the world. Bull riding, saddle bronc riding, bareback riding, steer wrestling, and other rodeo events demand not only skill but also present a high risk of injury: ranging from broken bones to life-threatening accidents.

Unlike athletes in football, basketball, or baseball, who typically have access to multimillion-dollar contracts, health benefits, and team-provided medical care, rodeo athletes operate in a very different reality. Most are self-employed, traveling from event to event, with no steady paycheck. The prize money they win in competitions is their primary source of income, but with an injury, they can be sidelined for months, and sometimes even for good. Additionally, rodeo athletes are responsible for their own health insurance and other benefits, which are often minimal due to the high-risk nature of their profession.

This can create a precarious situation for rodeo competitors. When a rodeo athlete is injured, they often face mounting medical bills, travel expenses, and the inability to provide for their families. The Justin Cowboy Crisis Fund (JCCF) helps bridge this gap by offering financial support, ensuring athletes can heal without the burden of financial distress.

Understanding the inherent risks of rodeo, Justin Boots partnered with the Professional Rodeo Cowboys Association (PRCA) and the Women's Professional Rodeo Association (WPRA) to create the fund. The goal was simple but essential: to provide rodeo athletes with financial assistance in their time of need, allowing them to focus on healing rather than worrying about bills or daily expenses.

By providing financial assistance during times of injury and hardship, the JCCF allows rodeo athletes to focus on what matters most: healing and returning to the sport they love. For over three decades, the fund has been a lifeline for thousands of rodeo athletes, offering hope and relief in their darkest hours.

As long as there are cowboys and cowgirls willing to risk it all in the rodeo arena, the Justin Cowboy Crisis Fund will be there, ensuring they are not alone when life takes a tough turn. Through the generosity of donors and the unwavering support of the rodeo community, the JCCF continues to uphold the values of resilience, community, and compassion that define the sport of rodeo.

The PRCA and Justin Boots underwrite all of the operational expenses of the JCCF, which allows 100% of the donations to go directly to the injured athletes. Since its founding, the JCCF has awarded nearly $9.5 million in assistance.

A COWBOY'S LAMENT

Nancy Taylor

He used to ride horses
In Rodeos each year
He doesn't now
Never touches a steer

The header, the heeler
He was part of the team
He isn't now
It's no longer his dream

In that white Western Hauler
He'd drive all night
To get to the next Rodeo
Before sunlight

He'd remove cover
Sing the Star-Spangled Banner
He still does
But only in the stands

He used to wear a starched white shirt
Wrangler and Purina patches on it
He doesn't now
He wishes those shirts still fit.

He puts his hat on the dresser
Brim up crown down
He doesn't want bad luck
Don't put it on his bed

He won his first buckle
A million years ago
He always wears it
Bet he always will

He wore tan suede chaps
Branded with his initials
They hang on a rack now
With his spurs and his rigging

He still chews Beech-Nut
Eats rare steak, drinks whiskey
He's stubborn that way
He knows that he shouldn't

He used to break buckle bunny's hearts
He'd kiss them and not tell
He doesn't now
He says, "oh, well…"

He used to drive an F-350
Black Dooley with tan guts
He wishes diesel wasn't so high
'Cuz he's not a rich guy

San Angelo and San Antonio in the spring
Cheyenne in their cool summer
They still call to him
He can't go…what a bummer

He used to be a Cowboy
He always will be
As the years go by
Nice guys finish dead but

Old Cowboys Never Die.

~ * ~ * ~

Nancy Taylor is a retired ordained Presbyterian Minister and lives in the hill country village of Wimberley, TX. Rev. Taylor served as pastor of small churches in small towns in Texas, Arkansas and Oklahoma for over 20 years. She has been a passionate writer for all of her adult life. In retirement, she has completed several writing projects, including a book of short stories, "The God-Awful Chair". She can be reached at ntay31@yahoo.com

RODEO PRAYER

Gary Every

When Grandfather Crazy Heart died in the year 1918, they took his two favorite ponies. They whispered in the horse's ears, "Grandfather loved you and he has need of you where he is going now."

The ponies stood with their heads to the east, tails to the west. They were magnificent animals. Had they been mine, I would have ridden them in the rodeo. They had such fierce hearts, they would have loved the competition, but Grandfather Crazy Heart did not know rodeo.

Grandfather Crazy Heart knew exactly where he was going to ride those horses in the afterworld and so did the people who buried him. Grandfather Crazy Heart would ride those horses, feathers tied in his hair, feathers tied in the horse's tail and mane, feathers waving in the wind. Crazy Heart would ride those fine horses in the afterworld. He would ride once again in the valleys where he had grown up, valleys where the oceans of prairie were filled with bison wading in the tall grass. They call this valley a reservation but that would have made Grandfather Crazy Heart Laugh. It is all just Earth, he would have said. like any other land. Perhaps a reservation is just a valley without buffalo.

I never knew where I was going to ride my favorite ponies. We went from rodeo to rodeo across the continent. The 1920's were a decade when rodeo roared. There were little arenas across western North America. Every rural Cowtown hosted at least one rodeo every year. My favorite ponies traveled everywhere, riding far more than they were ridden, standing inside my horse trailer, rolling along the highway, on their way to compete in another dusty cow town.

When Mother died, they did not allow us to bury her in our own way, according to our ancient traditions. They wanted my sweet mother laid out to rest in the Christian fashion. It was as if they wanted to send my mother away to an Indian boarding school in heaven. After my mother died, I felt her presence, her soul, her *nagi*, near me for four days. I felt as if some of her goodness was staying with me in a world where I must now do without her, without her wisdom and strength, without her breath upon my shoulder.

During the funeral, the priest talked about eternity. I told him we Indians did not believe in forever and forever. Only the rocks and mountains last and one day they too will be gone. There is always a new day coming and there is no such thing as forever.

"When it is my time to go," I said, "I want to go where my ancestors have gone."

The priest said, "Then, you will go to hell."

I told him, "I would rather fry beside a Sioux grandmother in Hades than sit on a cloud playing the harp next to a pale faced stranger."

The barbed wire fences appeared on the reservation when Congress passed the laws regarding allotment. The barbed wire boundaries defined what was and what was not the reservation. I was given sixty horses and sixty cows in return for relinquishing some of my land to grazing leases. I sold some of the livestock and bought a Model T Ford.

I drove the automobile all over, following the reservation rodeo circuit in Oklahoma, Gallup, Santa Fe, Saskatchewan and anywhere they put up an arena and a little prize money. It did not matter if the arena and prize money were small, I still showed up and rode.

I sold some more animals and bought everything in style for the Indian rodeos—big hat, fancy boots, and silver spurs. There were pretty girls at every rodeo. The pretty girls came in all colors, like a wonderful variety of flavors. I wanted all the girls to notice my big, champion belt buckle. My smile was always more handsome when I won.

Soon, all my livestock was gone, and I was the owner of a half dozen wrecked jalopies. I had traded in my herd of horses for a small collection of badly running automobiles. Often, I patched a car together with barely enough gas to reach the next small-town rodeo. I would need to win so I could use the prize money to fix the car, buy gas, and roll toward the next rodeo. Sometimes I won and sometimes I did not. Sometimes I left a broken truck behind a barn as I moved on to the next rodeo like leaving a sick horse in a stable. I littered the west with broken jalopies here and there. I also left behind a small scattering of children.

Even though I was the owner of many automobiles I was soon riding my hitchhiking thumb from mesa to mountain, highway to dirt road, rodeo to rodeo. I roamed. I became a wandering hippie Indian. My life was a find out. I went from reservation to reservation and everywhere I felt the spirits. I always burned a little sweet grass for them. I felt the touch of the spirits on my soul like a feather on a sore spot. Though I lived like a hobo I was visiting many old medicine men.

Every reservation I went to was filled with horses. I rode as many as I could. I watched them run and fell in love with every single one. There is nothing like watching a wild mustang run. They are the most beautiful creatures in the world, spirits of the wind. The long, long hair of their manes and tails flutters as they gallop like a thousand tiny, feathered wings.

The horse is the best thing the white man ever gave us. Equines first evolved in North America but migrated across the Bering Ice Bridge in the opposite direction and much earlier than the first Americans. The horses in North America went extinct and a species of horse in Mongolia spread across Eurasia. Horses did not return to the North American continent until Cortes brought them. It was the ill-fated Coronado expedition in 1540 which returned the horse to the American plains where they had roamed 10,000 years or so before. Many horses escaped from the expedition. Some horses were traded to the Native Americans. Other horses were stolen. The first hanging in North America took place in 1698 when the Spanish governor of New Mexico ordered two Native Americans hung for the crime of stealing horses.

Runaway horses from Spanish settlements repopulated the southern edge of the Great Plains and the population soon boomed to twenty million. Individual herds may have numbered in the tens of thousands. Horses from horizon to horizon, for as far as the eye could see. The Earth must have been a beautiful place in the days before the invention of barbed wire boundaries.

I searched for God or the Creator or whatever you want to call him, or her. I wandered everywhere during my search, asking questions of the land. I wanted the plants and stones to tell me their secrets. Everywhere I went there were always horses—typical bony reservation ponies. These horses had love and fire in their eyes, and they were always only half-tame. So fierce and proud; they would have made wonderful rodeo ponies, but it is better that they roamed free.

I had reached a point in my life where my herd of domesticated animals had been reduced to a pack of broken automobiles. Without a horse, the rodeo events I could enter were limited. I was bronc busting and bull riding. Both events were audience favorites, and the money was good, but it was hard on my body. As the years went by the injuries took longer to heal and some of them never healed completely. Eventually the aches and pains caught up to me and I retired from competing in the rodeo arena. My heart still felt young, but my bones were old.

I still traveled to rodeos, reservation rodeos in particular. I would patch up one of my jalopies enough to get to a rodeo and sometimes have to catch a ride back home. I made friends in many different distant places. Those friends, some of them human and some equine, made these distant arenas feel like home.

There is one rodeo I still visit every year, at Florence, Arizona, held on the weekend after Thanksgiving. It is a small rodeo in a small town on the edge of a reservation. The stands would be about the right size for a high school football game. The stands are filled with whites, Mexicans, Pima, and Apache, all of them traditional enemies of each other. They gather every year for this rodeo, for the love of the competition, for the love of the animals. Along the way, friendships are made.

One year, at a rural town rodeo whose directions included "turn onto the dirt road…" They mistook me for an elder and I was asked to deliver the blessing. Before every rodeo the human athletes are gathered, and a prayer is spoken. I was honored that they asked me. It meant I had been alive for a long time. It meant I was old.

I stood for a long time on the edge of a corral thinking about the words I would say. My arms were folded across one rail, and I had one boot on the lower railing. I watched the horses do what horses do, stand, sleep, eat, poop, prance, and play. I was hoping these creatures who ride the wind would help guide my words.

At last, the words came to me, and I left the corral railing. The human athletes gathered around me in a tight circle. There were many faces, women, men, black, brown, red, and white. When I began to speak my throat went dry. I was far more nervous than I expected.

I said, "Great Spirit, we pause; mindful of the many blessings you have bestowed upon us. We ask that you be with us at this rodeo, and we pray you will guide us through the arena of life. Help us to live our lives in such a manner that when we take our last ride to where the grass always grows green, and the water runs cool, clear, and deep, that you, as our last judge, will tell us our entry fees are paid."

When Grandfather Crazy Heart died, he rode his favorite ponies in the afterworld, in the bison laden valleys where he had grown up. When I die, gather up my favorite ponies from the distant lands where they graze. Load one into the trailer, drive to the next distant pasture, pick up the next horse, and then another long drive before you have all three. These horses are as beautiful as jewelry to me. They are like equine stones of turquoise, jet, and shell. Whisper in their ears and tell them I need them for one last arena.

When I die, bang the drum loudly until lightning flashes from the turquoise horse. The turquoise horse is terrifying. He stands on the upper circle of the rainbow, the sunbeam in his mouth for a bridle, hailstones for his teeth. Today I will win with the turquoise horse in the arena in the sky. The chute door swings open and the turquoise horse charges from the gate, hooves pounding the earth like war drums while the rodeo clowns dance. Dance little rodeo clowns, dance.

Gary Every is a journalist whose articles "Losing Geronimo's Language" and "The Apache Naichee Ceremony" won awards and are included in his anthology "Shadow of the OhshaD". He is the author of two published science fiction novellas "Inca Butterflies" and "The Saint and the Robot".

Mr. Every is currently the host of the literary reading program "The Poetry and Prose Project" on Mellow Mountain radio 780 AM, Sedona Arizona.

MEASURE OF A MAN

Madeline White

Ham needed to win that belt buckle.

He'd been thinking about it for weeks. He even had a dream last night where the judge handed it to him, and he attached it to his belt, big and shiny and silver, and everybody who walked past him knew he was a winner.

This belt buckle wasn't no two-bit tinny thing like the kind you could win with a bullseye on the county fair firing range, no sir. It was the real deal—shiny and thick and heavy in your hands, decorated with little turquoise stones and hard when you bit the corner so you knew it was real. Ham knew because Darryl had one.

Darryl had been Ham's age when he won it, and even though Darryl was a lot older than Ham now, he still had it up on the trophy shelf in the barn. It was his first belt buckle, but not his last, and Ham knew all a good cowboy needed was that first open door. That's what his Daddy always said, anyway. "Find you an opportunity, Hammy boy, and you stick your boot right in there before they can change their minds. Helton boys can start with nothin' and turn it to gold, and don't you ever forget it."

Helton boys turned everything they touched to gold, and that was the God's-honest truth. Everybody from Fort Bliss to San Angelo knew if you wanted a good cuttin' horse or the beef herd to match, Heltons were who you needed to talk to. The whole state and half of New Mexico knew Daddy and Darryl, knew if ya needed a good man you didn't have to look past 'em. And that could be Ham, too, right up there with 'em. As soon as he proved he was made of the same kinda stuff.

Standing up on the corral fence as Darryl started a fiery young mare, Ham pulled his ten-gallon hat down further to shield his eyes from the burning sun and watched his brother. Darryl was twelve years older than Ham and Momma and Daddy said Ham was "God's surprise gift". Darryl'd never acted too good for Ham, though. He was a good brother. Actually, he got Ham the hat he was wearin' right now. He gave it as a present last Christmas, tellin' Ham every good cowboy needs a good cowboy hat. It went nice with the boots Daddy got him, and Ham wore both proud as could be every chance he got.

Still, bein' Darryl's kid brother wasn't easy. Anywhere Ham stepped, Darryl'd walked there first, and his were big boots to fill, tell ya that for sure. Everybody loved Darryl. He was the four-time defendin' state cuttin' champ and he even got on the bulls now and then. He didn't do that good at bulls—not like he did on broncs—but he didn't embarrass himself neither, and that's what mattered, Darryl said.

"Ya gotta do your best, no matter whatcha do," Darryl said when they last dusted him off from a bull ride, talkin' funny past his busted lip, his left eye already startin' to swell up in the best shiner Ham ever saw. "Ain't gotta win, but ya gotta show 'em what yer made of. Us Heltons ain't quitters, and we ain't sore losers neither, ya hear?"

Ham had heard. But he wasn't gonna lose this time.

In the corral, the mare was givin' Darryl a real thrashin' about. Buckin' and spinnin' and kickin' her heels like mad. Daddy was on the other side of the ring, chewin' a cheek full of dip and watchin' Darryl with a deep crease like a fenceline between his eyebrows and the sweatband of his hat.

"Try an' settle 'er son, 'fore she hurts herself," he said, in that calm level voice he used when he was talkin' about horses.

Darryl didn't answer. The mare was really on one now, crow hoppin' in place while Darryl leaned back and let his body flop like a rag doll, absorbing the shock in his hips, same way Daddy always said to. Ham chewed on the toothpick Daddy gave him because, "dip's a filthy habit, boy, and I best never hear ya askin' about it again," and watched his brother with a mix of awe and jealousy.

Ham had never wanted to be anything worse than he wanted to be Darryl.

Finally, Darryl got the mare settled and after a few laps around the ring goin' way too fast, he got her stopped, ribs heavin' in the center of the pen. He rubbed her neck and slid off her back, his fingers leavin' white paths in the lather on her skin.

"Thanks for the advice, Pops," he said, cool as could be. "I never woulda thought to try and settle 'er." His voice was full of the kinda sass Daddy never woulda let Ham get away with, but he was grinnin', and Daddy didn't yell at 'im. "Guess that's why they call you the best of the best."

Daddy grinned too, his slap on Darryl's back makin' a smacking sound in the sweat soaking Darryl's plaid button-down. "And don't you forget it," he said, jokin' in that way he only ever did with Darryl. Ham watched and rubbed his thumbs over his store-bought buckle and thought he'd do anythin' to have Daddy talk to him like that. Daddy talked to Darryl like a man, but he talked to Ham like a kid.

Daddy walked around the mare's side and gave her a good scratch behind the ears before pullin' Darryl's saddle off for him and catchin' Ham's eye.

"Whatcha learn today, Hammy?" He asked, his voice gone soft. He slung the saddle over one arm and pulled Ham to him with the other. Daddy was always askin' Ham what he'd learned. He said whether you was in school or not, you oughta try to learn somethin' new every day. Bonus points if it was about horses. Or cattle. Cattle were good too, though to Daddy nothin' was as good as horses.

Even though Daddy was talkin' kid to him again, Ham grinned up at him, still glad to be included. "You ain't s'posed to stress 'em out when ya back 'em if you can help it. And if you can't, ya gotta settle 'em before they hurt themselves."

Daddy threw his head back and laughed, his big belly laugh that he rolled out on special occasions like cigars or the starched jeans without the holes in them. "You hear that, Darryl? Ham's got you beat! Maybe I oughta put *him* on the next one, if he keeps up like this!"

Ham swelled like a balloon and Darryl looked back with a smile. He grabbed the front of his hat with the hand not on the reins and tilted the brim towards his little brother. "Hey boss, why don't ya help me spray this mare down then, yeah? You help me get it done quick and I can help ya with your trainin' before Dad and I've gotta move the bull."

Ham rushed to join his brother, grabbin' the reins from him and leadin' the mare into the barn. She was mellowed out now and Ham ran the slicker over her after Darryl hosed her, pressin' sugar cubes into the soft velvet of her muzzle when Darryl wasn't lookin'.

After they put the mare back in the field, her brown and white belly swingin' merrily as she trotted to rejoin her herd, Darryl was true to his word and took Ham out to the trainin' barrel. It was a good one, one of them fancy kinds with a motor in it, bought new a few years ago. Darryl had learned on the old kind with the pull cords, but he said this was better. And Ham got to use it.

He could see the buckle on his belt now.

Darryl'd pulled off his usual straps and tied an old sheepskin to the barrel just for Ham. He gave Ham a boost and then walked around in a slow circle, lookin' over his brother and givin' him tips. Ham didn't sit back like Darryl did on the broncs. He leaned all the way forward, belly pressed hard to the barrel and metal-masked cheek in the wool, smellin' old hay and barn cats. His hands and legs both reached around the barrel, holdin' tight, fists full of fluff.

"Make sure ya grab it 'round the armpits," Darryl said, adjustin' Ham's arms. "On the real thing there'll be a lil dip here, between the shoulder and the barrel."

Ham listened intently, lettin' Darryl move his hands and then digging his fingers into the wool again. Darryl's hands moved to the facemask of Ham's helmet then, showin' him how to duck his head to save his neck. Darryl smelled like sweat and horse and red dust and Ham thought his big brother was maybe the realest cowboy there ever was. After Daddy at least.

Once Darryl got Ham all settled he asked, "Ya ready, kiddo?"

"I'm ready!"

Ham's heart thudded in his chest and he squeezed the barrel as tight as he could when Darryl pressed the button.

The barrel immediately ducked and spun, the force of it slinging Ham's insides against his ribs and threatening to fling him into the air. He buried his face against the dirty wool, helmet digging into the side of his temple, and held on for dear life as the barrel bucked and swung and twisted again and again and again like a tornado.

Then the barrel dipped forward abruptly and Ham lost his grip with his legs, sliding towards his hands even as the barrel spun again, dislodging him entirely and slinging him hard into the sand of the practice pit.

Ham hit the dirt like a rock, pain slamming up the right side of his body and sand filling his mouth. He stayed still for a moment, just like Daryll taught him, thinkin' about his body and makin' sure everything was where it should be. "Unless you're about to get trampled, ya never wanna jump straight up. If ya broke your neck or somethin', you'd paralyze yourself like that, right quick."

The barrel wasn't gonna trample him, so Ham took his second

to make sure he was okay. He was, just sore, his elbow stingin' from skiddin' on the sand. He dragged himself up and pulled off his helmet, dumpin' sand from his ear and spittin' to try and get it out of his mouth.

Darryl watched him, lettin' him dust himself off in peace before he held up the old yellow stopwatch they nicked from Daddy's desk. "Six seconds," he said.

Disappointment felt worse than the sand in Ham's shirt collar. He looked at the front of his jeans and brushed his hands over them as he grumbled, "felt longer."

Darryl laughed, but not at him. Just the way Darryl laughed sometimes when he knew somethin' Ham didn't. "Always does, kid."

Then Darryl smacked the barrel, the flat of his hand making a dull sound against the fleece. "Wanna go again?"

Ham did not want to go again. His shoulder ached and his elbow smarted and there was sand in his teeth and six seconds would never get him that belt buckle he needed so bad if he was ever gonna be half the man his brother was. Besides, it was only a barrel anyway, and how was he ever s'posed to get to be any good if he didn't get to practice on a—

"Hey boys, come help me unload the trailer, will ya?" Daddy called from somewhere in the barn, clearly lookin' for 'em. Ham wiped his eyes with his fists and looked at Darryl for an explanation, but Darryl just shrugged.

Ham trailed after his brother as they went out toward the driveway, secretly glad to get a break from the barrel before he had to fall off again and Darryl saw him maybe wantin' to cry.

Daddy had the trailer parked out by one of the calf pens, empty of calves right now (bein' mid-summer like it was), and even when he got closer to the trailer Ham couldn't tell what was s'posed to be in it. Daddy stepped around the back and he was grinnin' somethin' fierce, his blue eyes sparklin' under his wide brim.

"Got a present for you, Hammy boy," he said. Ham's heart lifted, but Daddy wouldn't say anythin' more. He and Darryl each grabbed a panel, blockin' off the chance of whatever it was escapin' 'round the side of the trailer instead of runnin' into the pen. They let Ham open the trailer door, reachin' up on his tiptoes and pullin' as hard as he could to get it unstuck.

It was all Ham could do to keep from jumpin' up and down

with excitement as they spilled out of the rig, and even that he could only manage because he didn't wanna spook 'em. There was fifteen of 'em, each more beautiful than the last, big and round and wooly, with delicate legs and placid faces. Ham scrubbed his eyes with his fists to make sure he was seein' right, and Daddy put his hand on Ham's head and tousled him even though he had on his ten-gallon hat.

"It was your momma's idea," Daddy said proudly. "She knows how bad you want that buckle."

Ham thought maybe he was gonna cry again and he hugged his dad so hard the hard lump of Daddy's Skoal can dug into his cheek. "Thank you, Daddy!" Ham said into the worn denim of his father's thigh.

"Thank your momma, too!" Daddy said, then he patted Ham on the shoulders. "And listen to Darryl, ya hear? He'll keep you safe."

~ * ~

Three weeks later, Ham was ready.

His Momma got him a brand-new pair of jeans for the occasion, crisp and dark blue with no itchy bits of hay stuck in the fabric. She'd helped him clean his boots, too, spreadin' a towel out on the carpet in the living room and putting on cartoons while they scrubbed the leather with a toothbrush and Ivory, then buffed it to shinin' with neatsfoot and beeswax. She'd pressed the collar of his good blue check shirt and helped him adjust the belt with the removable buckle.

Ham stood in the holding area behind the ring, listenin' to the roar of the crowd and the hammerin' of his own heart in his ears.

His hands were sweaty and he kept wipin' 'em on his jeans, wishin' they would stop before the sweat ruined his grip. There were three kids in front of him, each of them in outfits just as nice as his, numbers carefully pinned to their backs and helmets strapped on tight. One of them—Joey Blaine from school—had fancy new boots, black with green piping and snakes in the stitching. Jealousy and nerves tossed Ham's stomach, and he chewed on his lower lip.

The line of kids shuffled forward as the girl in front moved to the gate. Ham couldn't see the ring from where he stood, but he heard the slam of the gate opening followed by the whoops of the crowd as the girl and her sheep took off. Ham squinched his eyes closed and pictured the big orange numbers on the clock, trying to guess at how long the girl lasted by the sounds of the hollerin'.

The line moved forward again.

There was only him and Joey now. Joey looked back over his shoulder and shot Ham an orange-plastic-protected grin. Ham returned it and felt a little better.

The gate slammed, the crowd roared, and Joey stepped into the ring.

Ham didn't look at the line of kids behind him. He didn't listen to the crowd and try to time how long Joey lasted. He didn't even listen to Momma's last-minute tips, or the ringing in his own ears. He closed his eyes and pictured that belt buckle. Silver. Turquoise stones around the edges. A bucking ram and the words Ector County Fair 2024 in the center.

His belt buckle.

His destiny.

"Ya ready, Hamilton?" One of the clowns asked, putting a hand on his shoulder and guiding him forward. Ham opened his eyes.

He was ready.

The sand was soft and unstable under his feet as he stepped into the entryway of the arena. The lights were bright and hot, and sweat slicked his neck under the collar of his shirt. It tickled but he didn't want to wipe it and risk making his hands slippery.

He wiped his palms once more on his jeans and stepped up to the gate. Momma gave him a pat on the back and checked his helmet once more, wishing him luck. Ham could hardly hear her. He was staring at the gate. Red and ominous, a banging coming from inside, the sheep hankerin' to get out.

Ham swallowed hot spit, and then the clown lifted him up, hoisting him over the red pipe.

The ram was enormous. And he looked *mean*. The light of the devil glinted in his square-pupiled eyes, and his mouth twisted in a mocking grin. He was fatter than the sheep at home, harder for Ham to wrap his arms around. Ham tried his best anyway—he was a Helton boy after all. His face was sticky against the stinking body, and he tangled his fingers in the ratty white wool as best he could. The sheep squirmed as Ham wrapped his legs around its flanks, and the round barrel rolled under Ham's stomach. His hands were sweating again, he could feel it squeaky against the lanolin, but it was too late to wipe them.

"Good luck, Kid!" the clown cried, and he slammed open the gate.

The sheep lurched forward, running hell-for-leather across the deep sand of the ring, everyone whooping and screaming and windin' him up.

His body rocked as he ran, fat and wool rolling and wobbling, impossible to balance on, impossible to get a good grip.

Ham clenched his fists around handfuls of wool, but the lanolin was melting under the warmth of his hands, and what was sticky before was slick now, like a greased pig set loose in a cafeteria.

He fought desperately to pinch his knees, his ankles, his elbows and wrists, trying to keep himself pressed to the grooves in the rippling body. He tried to keep his belly and his face flat against the sheep, but he was slipping, rolling to the side now, losing his grip.

The crowd roared and the sheep's bucks sent bursts of pain through Ham's back and he had no idea how long the timer had been counting for.

Two seconds?

Ten?

A minute?

The muscles of his arms shook and his head began to flop as he lost his position and he thought maybe this was the longest anybody had ever rode a sheep before—impossibly long, each beat of his hammering heart an eternity of wool in his mouth and lanolin in his eyes.

The sheep banked hard to the left, Ham's body dangling to the right, and the two separated—strands of crimpy white coming off in Ham's hands as he hit the dirt *hard*.

Ham heard the horn as they stopped the clock, the hoots of the crowd, his family shoutin' his name, and the clowns going for the sheep.

He couldn't see the sheep so he got up without taking stock of himself, not wantin' to get trampled but also not wantin' to look hurt in front of his Momma.

Then he looked up at the clock.

4.86 seconds.

Sixth on the leaderboard.

Heartbreak.

Instant, overpowering heartbreak that hit him harder than the ground did and knocked his breath out just as good.

Then Momma was there, whiskin' him up into the bleachers. Daddy and Darryl were waitin' there, grins on their faces under their hats, splittin' sun-weathered skin with bright white teeth.

Ham could feel tears prickling at his eyes but he stubbornly blinked them back, not wantin' to look like a sore loser. Behind them, the mutton bustin' continued, more kids lining up and the crowd still yelling. But none of it mattered anymore. That belt buckle, that beautiful belt buckle, Ham's ticket to following in his brother's footsteps, was gone.

All that hard work and nothin' to show for it but a mouthful of sand and two handfuls of wool.

Then Darryl bent down with a smile, unclipping Ham's helmet and chucking him on the chin.

"Hey, you got the same time I did on my last bull ride!" Darryl said, tussling Ham's hair with a smile. "I better watch out—you're gonna be just like me kid, I just know it."

Then Darryl wiped the tears from Ham's cheeks with his thumb before anyone could see, and planted Ham's hat on his head before pulling him into a hug. And there, pressed against the red and black plaid of his big brother's chest, Ham realized he already knew exactly what kinda man he was gonna be.

~ * ~ * ~

Madeline is a southern transplant, farmer and artist living in rural NY with her partner and horses. By day she squeezes wool art and animal care into the space left over from her corporate grind, and by night she writes grimdark fiction as a break from her cottagecore reality.

Her work has appeared in the *Reptiles* issue of Honeyguide Magazine, as well as *Sincerely, Departed* by Voices from the Mausoleum, with *Howling For You* upcoming from the same press. She also has upcoming fiction and recipes in *Cursed Cooking* by Cat Eye Press, and believes everything is better fried.

Find her on Instagram and TikTok as @light_in_the_grimdark and on Twitter as @LightInGrimdark

THE FLYING CHANGE

Evalyn Lemon

In the Northwest, where Oregon, Washington and Idaho come together, the desert forms a motionless landscape that stretches in all directions with an astounding, disconcerting sameness. There are no markers for distance traveled. The near sagebrush is the same as the far sagebrush, and in between is always more sagebrush. Only the numbers on the odometer advance.

Smokey Monroe drove his old truck across that desert, classic country music playing on the radio, windows open to the dry wind. He tapped rhythm to the music against the edge of the steering wheel and thought, once again, how he really should learn to play guitar. Then, once again, the engine of the old red Ford sputtered, hesitated, and died. He switched off the key and let the truck coast onto the shoulder. The radio went dead right in the middle of an old George Jones tune, but Smokey kept singing to the end of the verse. He knew the words as well as he knew what was wrong with the Ford. Besides, it was just rude to leave The Old Possum hanging in mid-verse like that. As the truck rolled to a stop, Smokey felt the sun's heat beat into him, and breathed in the scents of dust and sage as the enormous silence of the desert replaced the noise of the radio.

The temperature gauge on the dash registered in the red, and the aroma of antifreeze filled the cab. That old slow leak in the water pump had caught up with him again; nothing to do but let the engine cool a bit before he added water. He settled deep into the well-worn pocket in the truck seat, gazed out across the sage flat and let last night's ride in Lewiston come back to him.

~ * ~

His first draw had been a saddle bronc with a good kick, but Smokey had ridden it out. His spurs raked front to back across the bay horse's hide as it pitched and bucked around the arena, doing its best to lose him. He rode loose in the saddle, his left hand high, as he whipped and swayed with the movements of the horse. When the buzzer sounded, he twisted his body toward the pickup rider and bailed off the bay. He swung across the back of the pickup horse and landed on his feet in the dirt on the other side. He doffed his hat in response to the clapping, cheering crowd. The announcer's voice boomed out over the loudspeaker: "Smokin' Joe Monroe from Burns, Oregon. Well, look at that, boys—the best points so far tonight. This cowboy could win a prize." Smokey sauntered from the arena with a limp that was only partly for show.

In the bareback event his draw had been a rangy gray gelding, a horse who was not having a fun day at the rodeo. The horse fought the chute, rearing up on his hind legs. He struck the rails with his front hooves, driving the cowboy away twice. Smokey finally got astride the horse and tugged his hat down tight. He nodded to the gateman. The gate swung wide and the gray lunged from the chute. The horse hit the ground, grunted hard and launched himself into the air, all four feet off the dirt of the arena. The cowboy drove his legs forward then pulled his knees up toward his chest, raking his spurs along the horse's shoulders. The big gray mule-kicked both back legs out behind, his head straight down between his forelegs.

Smokey leaned back and raked him again. The big horse squealed and see-sawed up on his hind legs, threatening to go over backward. The cowboy pushed his weight forward, yelling curses at the horse. The gray's front feet hit the ground with a thud that jarred every bone in the man's body. With barely a pause the horse leaped straight up in the air, thrashing his body like a fish fighting the hook. The crowd roared. The rider spurred and cursed and prayed for the buzzer. Every muscle in his body screamed with strain. Every bone ached for mercy. The horse put his head down again and crow-hopped twenty punishing feet across the arena.

The pickup men were closing in for the end when Smokey lost his seat. His bad leg wouldn't hold. When the horse went left, he went right. For an instant he had the heady sensation of being completely airborne. He heard the collective gasp of the crowd and remembered to tuck his chin before he hit the ground. He landed in an untidy heap on top of his hat.

The crowd politely applauded his effort. The pickup man brought his horse alongside. "You okay, Smokey?" he asked.

"Hell, yes," Smokey said and turned to the crowd and waved. They were already focused on the gates, ready for the next rider. He bent to retrieve his hat from the dust and made his way across the chewed surface of the arena. The gray loped past as pickup riders hazed him back to the holding pens. Clods flew from the horse's hooves raining one last indignity on the limping cowboy.

The buck-off had put him out of the running for all-around, so he had drawn his winnings from the first ride and headed for the parking lot.

~ * ~

The cooling truck made a gargling noise that drew Smokey's attention back to the here-and-now. He got the water jug from the back of the truck and propped the hood up with the stick he carried for just this purpose. The cap was still hot, but he knew from long experience gurgling meant the radiator had cooled enough to be safe.

He dribbled water from the jug into the radiator slowly, letting the coils fill. Then he got down on his knees to check under the engine. The leak from the water pump seemed no worse than normal. The engine purred to life at the turn of the key, just like always. He steered back onto the highway and continued across the desert.

Early next morning, a loud noise outside the pickup startled him awake. He sat up too quickly and smacked his head on the inside of the canopy.

The noise was a motorcycle in the parking lot of the motel where Smokey couldn't afford a room. The canopy on the back of the pickup truck was his home-away-from-motel and contained his sleeping bag with a foam pad, and his championship saddle with "All-Around Cowboy, Calgary Stampede" stamped on the skirt with a year that was a long time ago. Next to that was his worn old bucking rig, a duffle with three changes of shirts and jeans, his riding gloves, and a shaving kit with twenty dollars stashed in the lining.

With his only towel over his shoulder and the shaving kit under his arm, he used the bathroom at the gas station next door to freshen up. The glow of the single bulb cast a gray tint over his skin, turning every crease in his face to a shadowed fold. The water in the sink ran for some time without getting warm, so he splashed cold water on his face and scraped the towel across the stubble of his beard.

In the hotel café, hovering over his second cup of coffee, he contemplated his ibuprofen level. He had paid his fee to ride in Caldwell the next day and was signed up for Boise on the weekend.

Not for the first time, he felt as tired as his aging truck, held together with stubbornness, long experience and odd bits of wire.

As he hesitated before shaking pain medication into his palm, a shadow fell across the table. He looked up into a familiar face, lined with wrinkles and topped by a shiny bald scalp that reflected the morning light like a new coin.

"Smokin' Joe Monroe," the man declared, tossing his hat onto the table. "How the hell are ya?"

Smokey stood to grasp the gnarled and weather-beaten hand of his friend. "Red Shannon. I'm fair. How's yourself?" The two men shook hands hard and grinned at each other for a long moment.

"Sit down," Smokey invited, gesturing to the other side of the booth.

"Saw you ride last night." Red signaled the waitress for coffee. "You still do pretty good, for an old man."

Smokey snorted. "And feelin' it this morning." He juggled the pill bottle from hand to hand.

"I figured you would be here this morning, like the old days. Where you headed next?"

"Saddle bronc tomorrow in Caldwell." Smokey drained the last of his coffee and slipped the ibuprofen back into his pocket. The waitress refilled his cup when she delivered Red's coffee.

"What are you up to these days?" Smokey asked. "I haven't seen you around since that wreck a couple years back."

Red's eyes crinkled in his weathered face, and he ran a big, knuckled hand over his naked head. "The bull won," he said, raising his cup in salute. "My daughter talked me into retiring."

"I heard that. Couldn't believe you gave up bulls for a rockin' chair."

Red grinned. "No chair. Got a regular job at a Western store, talking folks into buying fancy gear. I work a couple days a week and play with my grandkids the rest of the time." His eyes twinkled. "I keep an old horse out at my place, teach the kids to ride. I leave the rough stuff to you young bucks."

Retirement, Smokey thought. *Turned-out for good.* But a man needs a little more to fall back on than a worn-out Ford, a well-used bucking rig and past glory. There had been a time when the future seemed sure, and the rides would be good forever. That was before Pendleton four years ago, that big roan horse and weeks in rehab with pins and plates in his leg. But hell, he could still ride. Plenty of time yet for that last go-round.

Red was fishing in his wallet. "You meet all sorts of people workin' retail," he said. "I've got a customer from over at Emmett. He breeds and trains quarter horses for the track. Comes in pretty regular to talk horses and rodeos and such." The old cowboy extracted a business card from his wallet, studied it for a moment, turned it in his fingers. He laid it on the table between them. "He's lookin' for a trainer."

Smokey looked at the card, then at Red.

Red poked the card with a finger, nudging it across the table. "I told him I knew a fella. A good hand with a horse. But I didn't know if he was ready to turn-out since he's still ridin' in the money." He drained his coffee and got to his feet, one joint at a time. "I'm workin' today, so I better get movin'."

Smokey rose to face his friend and the two of them shook hands again. Red ambled out the door and Smokey dropped money next to his coffee cup. He left the business card lying on the table.

He was set to walk away. Then with the same twist that got him off the plunging back of a bucking horse and behind the saddle of the pickup man, he reached back and snagged the card off the table.

Out in the desert it all looks the same; the only thing that changes are the numbers on the odometer. But at some point, a line is crossed. Weathered old fence posts and fallen down barns come into view, then fade behind. A mailbox flashes by. And closer and closer all the time, the green blush of cultivation.

The Flying Change first appeared in
Mosaic, An Association of Writers Anthology – 2017
Reprinted by permission of the author

~ * ~ * ~

Evalyn Lemon began writing stories as soon as she learned to arrange words into sentences. As an adult, and gifted with a short attention span, she writes short fiction, most of it with a Pacific Northwest flavor.

She graduated from the University of Oregon with a BA in English, and now lives between the South Umpqua River and the Cascade Mountains, in the company a standard poodle—LuLu, and two kittens—Bonnie and Clyde.

CHERRY BLOSSOMS IN THE SPRINGTIME

David Lee Summers

Caleb Brown sat in the living room of his little homestead beside the rough-hewn wooden coffin that contained the body of his young wife. His body was so wracked with sobs he barely noticed the tremor that rocked the house and dislodged a slipper from Tabitha's foot. A few minutes later, his young son Sherman appeared, framed in the living room's doorway. Looking up, Caleb wiped away a tear and tried to conceal a snuffle behind the sleeve of his woolen jacket. "What's the matter son?" he asked.

"Something woke me up," the young boy said. He rubbed his arms vigorously together and looked at the body of his mother in the coffin. His eye fell on the slipper sitting beside her foot. "Her feet are going to get cold," he said matter-of-factly.

Caleb noticed the slipper and his eyebrows came together. He reached down and straightened her foot, the coldness of it bringing a fresh tear. He sniffed and wiped it away, doing his best to be brave for his son.

"Can I put her slipper back on her foot?" Sherman asked, frowning and near tears himself.

Caleb nodded and fell back into the flower-patterned armchair —Tabitha's favorite—while the boy reached into the coffin and gently replaced the slipper. Sherman turned to his dad, climbed into his lap, buried his face into his shoulder and cried. A few minutes later, both Caleb and his son fell into a deep sleep.

~ * ~

The funeral was on Easter Sunday, 1934. Caleb, Sherman, and Tabitha's family were gathered in the tiny cemetery in Des Moines, New Mexico, a little farming and ranching town on the plains near the Colorado and Texas borders. The wind howled so loudly Caleb could barely hear the words of the Baptist minister. In many ways he was just as glad. He wanted to be alone with his grief. Instead, he kept catching Tabitha's sister and brother stealing glances at him. Tabitha's father—a stern man with fiery red hair—glared at him as the minister's voice droned on, competing with the wind. Avoiding his father-in-law's gaze, Caleb looked toward the grave of his own mother who died twelve years before and wished she were there to comfort him.

He couldn't have told anyone how long he stood there staring, but a tugging at his coattail finally broke his reverie. He looked down and saw Sherman. Caleb knelt down and drew his son close to hear what he had to say.

"Dad, what's that funny cloud over by Mount Capulin? Is it a tornado?"

Caleb turned his head and looked at the cone-like mountain responsible for much of the basaltic rock that covered their corner of Northeastern New Mexico. "It's not a tornado," he whispered. His eyebrows came together. At first he thought it was the strangest looking dust plume he'd ever seen. Then he realized what he was seeing wasn't dust; it was more like the plume of smoke from a factory's smokestack being blown in the wind. "I think it may be a forest fire," he said.

Just then, he felt a tapping on his shoulder. He looked up into the eyes of his father-in-law. The wind had died down enough he could hear the minister saying, "Ashes to ashes, dust to dust."

Caleb stood and walked over to the gravesite, picked up a small handful of dirt and tossed it onto his wife's coffin and said a quiet good-bye as the dirt thunked hollowly on the wooden lid. He then turned and took his son's hand and led him to the cemetery gates where their old Model-T Ford was parked. Without looking up at any of Tabitha's family, he turned the crank on the front of the car until it clattered to life. He climbed in, put it in gear and drove back to the homestead.

Once there, he stepped out of the car and looked at two cherry trees that had blossomed out in vivid pink. He took a deep breath and let it out slowly thinking how much Tabitha had loved those trees, then closed his eyes. A moment later, he turned and looked at his son, who had curled up in the passenger seat and fell asleep; exhausted both from the overwhelming emotions surrounding his mother's death and standing out in the windy, dusty cemetery. Caleb stepped over, picked up the boy and carried him inside to bed.

~ * ~

That afternoon, family and friends gathered at the homestead. Most brought food, but Caleb found much of it didn't appeal to him. During the Great War, he had been a cook. He had started in mess halls, but the officers soon discovered his work. Before long, he found himself cooking for General Pershing. When the war ended, the general asked him to stay on, but his parents said they needed his help with their homestead, so he returned to New Mexico. His mother died only five years after the war and his father five years after that, leaving him with a farm too hard to work alone, in a town too small to provide any other work.

He occasionally made some money from bull riding competitions at the rodeo. Besides cooking, it was the one thing he was good at. In fact, some of the local ranchers were organizing a spring rodeo for the following weekend in the town of Springer. Caleb sighed. He didn't feel much like bull riding in the wake of his wife's death. At least he had his pension from the Army.

As people milled about, trying to find words to comfort one another, Caleb stared out the window at Mount Capulin, avoiding conversation. The wind had died down, but the strange plume of dust or smoke still hung over the mountain. If it was a forest fire, it was an odd one that didn't seem to be growing. A hand on Caleb's shoulder startled him. He turned around and found himself staring into the icy blue eyes of his father-in-law, Sherman Wallace. Without a word, the large man took Caleb by the elbow and led him outside to the front porch.

Once there, Caleb fumbled for words, but Wallace held up his hand. "Your words canna bring her back," he said. "It's your son I want to speak about."

"What about him?" Caleb looked through the screen door and saw his son, now awake, sitting in a chair, eating a ham sandwich.

"I'm concerned for his well-being," the boy's namesake said. "I dinna think it's right that a man without a job should raise a boy all alone."

Caleb looked into his father-in-law's eyes. "What choice do I have?"

"Let the boy move in with Emma and I while you look for work. Or, better yet, let him go to Raton where he can stay with Ethel and Glen. It's a bigger town than Des Moines. The change of scene would do the boy good."

Caleb thrust his hands into his pockets and looked down at the wooden planking of the porch. "I don't want to give up my boy, Mr. Wallace."

"I'm not askin' ye to give him up," Wallace said. "I'm only askin' ye to give him a stable home until ye get money so you can provide for him."

"I have a pension from the army," Caleb said, shaking his head. "I'm a good bull rider. Between the two, there's money."

"Aye," Wallace snorted derisively. "Charity from the government and gambling are not the same as the money you can make from honest work."

"Honest work?" Caleb asked, looking up at last. "I have the farm. How much more honest is that?"

"And look at the state it's in." Wallace's eyes narrowed as he scanned the countryside. "All ye've got is a small crop of corn and two cherry trees. That's not enough."

"There's my pension…my winnings…"

"Which keep you in beer and booze!"

"I don't drink…much," Caleb said as he stormed down the porch steps.

"Between your drinking and your bull riding, you worried my Tabby sick," Wallace called, barreling along behind him. "She died so young because she constantly tended to you."

Caleb whirled around on the big man. "Tabitha died of Rheumatic fever," he shouted. "It wasn't my fault!"

Wallace's jaw was set, and he stared at his son-in-law for several minutes. "I wish I could believe that," he breathed at last. The older man turned and started back to the house. "I wish I could believe you were the best man to take care of my grandson."

Caleb rushed forward and grabbed Wallace by the shoulder and spun him around. "There's nobody better to watch my son. Nobody. You wait and see. I'll get a job. I'll get money."

Wallace heaved a deep sigh. "I hope you're right." He looked to the ground for a long moment. When he looked up, he seemed more composed and the color had drained from his cheeks. "If ye don't get a job, just promise me ye'll take him to stay with Ethel and Glen. He would enjoy spending time with his aunt and uncle."

"I'll think about it," Caleb said.

"That's all I ask."

Caleb shoved his hands into his pockets and watched his father-in-law walk away. He had no idea where he would find a job, but he knew how he could get some money. He could compete in the rodeo the following weekend. He didn't feel like it, but if it was the only way he could keep his son, he would.

~ * ~

The next morning, Caleb woke before dawn, did his chores around the homestead, then came inside and cooked breakfast for Sherman. The boy awoke a short time later and came into the kitchen. "How do you feel, son?"

"I miss mom," he said as Caleb placed a plate of bacon, eggs, and grits in front of him.

"I know," Caleb said. "Do you feel like going to school today?"

The boy lifted a piece of bacon to his mouth and chewed it contemplatively while looking around at the kitchen. At last, he looked into his father's eyes. "Yeah," he said. "It'd be better than sitting around here; better than doing chores."

Caleb nodded. "I know what you mean," he said as he dug into his own breakfast.

The two finished their breakfast in silence, then cleared the table. Sherman went to his room to get dressed and gather his schoolbooks. Caleb poured a cup of coffee and went out to the front porch where he saw the smoke plume on Capulin had grown. As he sipped his coffee, he wondered whether the volunteer fire brigade from the village of Capulin at the mountain's base needed help combating the blaze. He felt his heart pound at the prospect. First, he would drive to Springer and sign up for the rodeo, come back to Des Moines for lunch, then drive out to Capulin to see if he could help with the fire. It was a good plan. Maybe someone else on the fire brigade or at the rodeo would have a job for him.

Sherman appeared at the door and Caleb drained his coffee. He set it down on the porch railing then stepped over to the Model T and cranked the engine over. As he and Sherman climbed into the car, there was a rumble and the rickety car began to tremble more than usual. "Maybe I'd better get this thing into the garage," Caleb said under his breath.

Sherman pointed toward the porch. Caleb turned and saw the empty cup rattling toward the edge of the railing. It tumbled off and shattered against the rock-hard ground.

"Another tremor?" Caleb asked under his breath.

"Aren't you going to sweep it up?" Sherman asked.

Caleb looked at his pocket watch and shook his head. "No time. We're running late as it is." With that he released the brake and steered the car out onto the road toward town.

An hour later, Sherman was in class and Caleb was pulling up to Mack Levine's ranch house in Springer. He climbed out of the car and made his way to the nearby corrals. He found Levine atop a horse, giving instructions to two of his cowhands. When the two rode off, Levine turned his attention to Caleb. "Well, howdy," the rancher said. He dismounted and clasped Caleb's hand. "How are you doin', Caleb? Sorry I couldn't make it to the funeral yesterday. Between getting things ready for the rodeo and the spring roundup, I've been busier than you can believe."

"I *can* believe it," Caleb said. He looked around at the corrals and took in the smells of manure. It seemed stronger than normal. Of course, the government had been trying to get farmers to switch to chemical fertilizers, so they weren't hauling as much of the manure away as they once did. "Say, any chance I can sign up for the bull riding competition this Saturday?"

"Are you sure you're up to it?" Mack asked. His mustache drooped, framing his concerned frown.

"It'll help me take my mind off things," Caleb said.

Mack nodded, understanding. "Would you like to make a trial run? Tornado's got a bull rope on and he's ready and rearin' to go. I can get a couple of the hired hands over and we can see how you do."

Caleb pursed his lips and nodded. "Yeah, I think a ride would do me good about now."

"We got gloves and chaps in the shed over there." Mack pointed to a nearby building. "Get yourself ready and I'll go round up a couple of the boys."

As Caleb went to the shed, he found himself remembering Wallace Sherman's words about Tabitha worrying herself sick over his riding. Caleb shook his head. He knew that just couldn't be true. Tabitha always supported him; she always cheered him on. As he donned the chaps, he realized she wouldn't be there anymore. He took a deep breath, then removed his pocket watch, so it wouldn't be damaged.

Just before he put on the gloves, he rubbed his eyes, hoping tears wouldn't spill out in front of Mack Levine and his ranch hands. He sniffed and thrust his hands into the gloves, then stepped out into the warm New Mexico sunshine.

He stepped over to the corral where Mack Levine and two of his men stood. Tornado was in the pen. He was shuffling his feet and his skin twitched here and there. "He's a bit feisty after yesterday's windstorm," Mack explained. "You sure you're ready to try this?"

"Ready as I'll ever be," Caleb said, with a clenched jaw.

Mack and one of the hands helped him over the fence and onto Tornado's back. Caleb grabbed the bull rope and the other ranch hand opened the gate. Tornado shot out, anxious to get Caleb off his back. True to his name, Tornado spun around in rapid circles. Caleb held on to the rope and did his best to find Tornado's rhythm and ride with it. He tried not to think about the possibility of falling. It never bothered him before because Tabitha had always been there for him. Her face came to his mind and for just a moment he lost concentration. He found himself off Tornado's back. His feet hit the ground with a crunch and he felt them grind in the dirt as Tornado led him around a bit before he let go of the rope. One of Mack Levine's hands led Tornado away and the other rushed up to Caleb, leading him to the side of the pen.

Mack Levine stood to the side, holding a watch and shaking his head. "That was only seven seconds, Caleb." His mustache drooped. In spite of the pain in all his joints, Caleb could practically feel the rancher's disappointment. "Your style was pretty good, but something happened. Tornado shook you awfully easy."

"I lost concentration," Caleb managed to say.

"You better think long and hard about Saturday," Mack said. "I'll put you down for a ride, but I hope you can concentrate better then. It's awfully easy to get trampled or gored out there if you're not thinking."

"I know," Caleb sighed. "Thanks for letting me have a ride."

"No problem," Mack said.

~ * ~

There was one bar in Des Moines, New Mexico in 1934: The Roadrunner. Though many avoided it because it served alcohol, it had a decent grill. Caleb shuffled in soon after the bar opened at noon. He plunked two bits on the counter. "Hey, Bud, how about a burger and…a beer."

Bud MacDonald stepped out from the kitchen. He looked down at the two coins on the counter and silently pushed them back toward his friend. He then reached into the icebox under the bar, retrieved a bottle of beer, and set it down in front of Caleb. "Man, you look beat," Bud said, his eyebrows furrowed.

Caleb looked into the bottle and sighed. "I was over in Springer," he said. He told Bud about how he only managed seven seconds on Tornado. He then told him about the conversation with his father-in-law.

Bud reached out and put his hand on Caleb's shoulder. "The day after your wife's funeral isn't the best time to go out and get on the back of a bull. Maybe you should take some time off and get yourself together. You've got your pension…"

"Charity from the government," Caleb snorted.

"That's just your father-in-law talking."

"You wouldn't have a job for me, would you?" Caleb looked back toward the kitchen.

"I wish I could afford to hire you." Bud shook his head. "You know, if I were you, I'd pack up Sherman and get out of this Hellhole. A cook like you could get a job anywhere. Go north to Denver or East to Amarillo. There's nothing holding you here."

"But how do I get the money to go there. It would take all of a pension check to buy a train ticket for Sherman and me. There'd be nothing left for a hotel room when I got wherever it was I was going."

"You're signed up for the rodeo."

"But I won't get any money from that unless I can hold on for better than eight seconds." Caleb sighed and looked into his beer. "I haven't done this badly since I was a kid."

"Don't be so hard on yourself," Bud said. "This is a hard time. You'll do better this weekend. I know you will." With that, Bud went out back to check on the fire.

Caleb sat alone in the quiet and dark of the bar, glad to be alone for a time. He kept staring at the bottle of beer, never quite bringing it to his lips; the words of his father-in-law about his reputation as a drinking man resonated in his mind. The door at the back of the bar opened and Caleb looked up, expecting to see Bud. Instead, it was Bud's nineteen-year-old daughter, Vinita.

She came around the bar and sat on a stool next to him. "Mr. Brown, I'm sorry I didn't get to say anything yesterday at the funeral. I'm so sorry…"

Caleb reached out and took Vinita's hand. "I know," he whispered. "Talk to me about something else, though. My mind keeps swirling around Tabitha and I can't get the picture of her body in the coffin out of my mind. Talk to me about life, not death."

Vinita nodded and swallowed hard. Her eyes flitted back and forth as she thought. "I went out to Johnson Mesa the other day. You should see the cherry trees. They're all over the place up there and alive with color. It would do your heart good."

He squeezed her hand and let go as Bud came back in with the hamburger. "Thanks, Vinita," he said with a sigh. "I'll go do that."

"Hey," Bud said, "Have you seen that forest fire up on Capulin? I noticed it yesterday, but it seems like it's growing."

Caleb nodded. "I've been thinking about going out to the village to see if the volunteer fire department needs any help." He picked up a fork, then poked at the fried potatoes on his plate.

"It might do you good to help on the fire brigade," Bud agreed. "It would take your mind off of things…but if you go, be careful. You want to be in good shape when you ride in the rodeo."

Both looked up as the door opened. A thin man with a tweed suit and glasses stepped inside. He sat down on the empty stool on the other side of Caleb. "Do you serve food?" he asked.

"Best sandwiches in Union County," Caleb said holding up his hamburger.

The man pulled out a silver dollar and placed it on the counter. "That looks good, I need one as quickly as you can. There's trouble brewing and I need to get on my way."

Bud picked up the silver dollar and reached into his apron to pull out fifty cents change. The man waved him off. "Just get going," he said impatiently. "Keep the change."

"Thank you," Bud said as he hurried outside to place another hamburger on the grill.

Caleb took a bite of his hamburger then offered his hand to the man. "Name's Caleb Brown," he said. "What's going on?"

The man shook Caleb's hand. "I'm Luke Anderson with the

School of Mines down in Socorro. We've been measuring tremors for over a week now. Correlating our data with scientists up in Golden and those at Texas Western, we've pinpointed the source up here in Northeastern New Mexico. On the drive through, I see Capulin's gone active again."

Vinita gasped and Caleb sat his hamburger down on the plate. "What?" he asked. "You mean to say that's not just a forest fire up there?"

"I wish it was," Anderson said. "I'm here to take some measurements, but if this is as bad as I think it is, I think the towns of Capulin, Des Moines, and Folsom are all in danger."

"What can we do?" Vinita said.

"Do?" Anderson asked. "Tell your friends and family to get out of here. If that mountain goes, it's going to be like Pompeii around here."

Caleb pushed his potatoes around with his fork, his brow furrowed. Memories of the war came back to him. Even though he hadn't been a soldier in the field, the sounds of explosions still haunted his dreams. After the war, before he returned home, he traveled to Pompeii and saw the ash and lava field that buried an entire city. He thought about the cherry trees, both in front of his homestead and the ones Vinita told him about and thought about them burning to the ground. He looked at the mountain-like cone of potatoes on his plate. "What exactly is going on inside the volcano?" he asked dreamily.

"Under the surface of the Earth, magma is building pressure. Once the pressure gets to a critical point, it'll explode through the weakest point."

"Like the Huns through Denmark," Caleb remarked. He pointed to the center of his potato model. "I'm guessing the weakest point is here, at the center of the mountain?" he asked.

"Most likely," Anderson agreed. "In the crater. When it goes, ash, cinders and lava will blow out. The ash and cinders are your biggest immediate danger out here in Des Moines. However, if the volcano goes for several days, the lava flows could reach out here. In ancient times, lava did cover this area."

"How do you know that?" Vinita asked, eyes wide from both fascination and horror.

"I can tell from the red rock that covers this portion of the state. Driving in, you can see it all over the place," Anderson explained as Bud emerged from the back with a plate containing a hamburger and home fries.

"What if we made a new weak spot?" Caleb asked. He pointed to his potato mountain again—this time at one edge. "Say up in the northwest, away from the villages."

Anderson picked up his hamburger and took a mouthful, then chewed while pondering the idea. He then reached down and took a drink from his bottle of beer. "Interesting idea," he said, "but how would you create a weak spot?"

"Blast the side of the mountain." He took a scoop of the potatoes and popped them in his mouth. "We could get dynamite from the coal mines in Raton."

"I don't know if we have enough time...or money for that matter. I doubt the mines in Raton would just give us the dynamite we'd need...and we'd need a lot," Anderson said dubiously. "You've got a great idea in theory, but I don't know how we can make it a reality."

Caleb looked down at his plate again. Dejected, he reached down and picked up his own hamburger and chewed it slowly. Bud picked up a glass and began wiping it for lack of anything else to do. Vinita looked sadly to her father, then her mouth fell open. "What about that new chemical fertilizer they've been trying to get the farmers to use in place of cow manure?"

"What does that have to do with anything?" Bud asked.

"There's all kinds of warnings on it, saying not to store it near flame and stuff. It's supposed to be pretty explosive."

Bud set the glass down and inclined his head, looking at his daughter. "Do you remember what this new fertilizer is supposed to be made of?"

"Phosphorus, ammonia, nitrogen, stuff like that...I think," Vinita said.

"What does that matter?" Anderson asked, his curiosity piqued in spite of his skepticism.

"There's pounds and pounds of chemical fertilizer around and I heard tell Old Man Seaton was getting set to blast a well," Bud explained. "He has a little dynamite. Not enough to blast a hole in a mountain..."

"...but enough to set off some bags of fertilizer for sure," Caleb said. He stood up from the bar stool and looked at Vinita. "Pick up

Sherman from school. Take him into Raton where you'll be safe. You can stay with my sister-in-law, Ethel." He looked at Bud. "Close up the bar and we'll take your truck. We've got to collect some fertilizer."

Luke Anderson shook his head. "Your scheme might not work. You could blow yourselves up and not save anything."

"We won't know unless we try," Caleb said.

"What are you going to do?" Vinita said.

"We're going to try to save the cherry blossoms," Caleb said. When he looked up, Bud was already grabbing his jacket.

~ * ~

The first thing Bud and Caleb did was stop off at the sheriff's to let him know about the volcano. The sheriff nodded and said he'd spread the word—start getting people moving toward Raton and Amarillo. The two friends didn't mention their plans to try to save the town. It was likely the sheriff would try to stop them.

On their way to the first farm, Bud looked at Caleb. "So, why do you give a damn? You don't have anything here anymore. Tabitha's gone. Wallace wants to take your son away from you. You should just get out of here while the getting's good."

"Maybe," Caleb said, "but this isn't about me. It's about the people who built up farms and lives around here. It's about good people like Old Man Seaton and Mack Levine. It's about the memory of my mom and dad and Tabitha. She may be gone, but her mom and dad are still here."

"Yeah," Bud said, "but her mom and dad are the ones who want to take Sherman away from you."

"What do I tell Sherman when he grows up and asks why his grandparents moved away, why they couldn't make a living?" Caleb shook his head. "I may not like Wallace much right now but all he knows is farming. If his farm was destroyed, his life would be over just as much as if he burned in the lava itself. For Tabitha's sake and for Sherman's I can't just let that happen. I can start over somewhere else. They couldn't." He looked over at his friend. "I couldn't let your livelihood be destroyed either."

Bud shook his head as he turned down the road to the first farm. "Now that prohibition's been lifted, I could open a bar anywhere."

They pulled up to the farmhouse and knocked on the door. Mrs. Seaton answered and told the men her husband was out in the field.

They saw him working the field with a horse-drawn plow and ran out to him. They pointed up to the mountain and explained the situation.

"You mean that isn't just a forest fire?" he asked.

Bud and Caleb shook their heads then told him about their plans to vent the volcano with fertilizer and dynamite. Old Man Seaton looked around his field with his hands on his hips. "This farm ain't much," he said, "but I'd sure hate to have it burned up." He led them back to the barn where he helped them load the pickup with bags of fertilizer. Then he retrieved several sticks of dynamite.

"You better clear on out of here," Caleb said. "There's no guarantee this will work."

"My wife has relatives over in Raton. We'll stay with them until this blows over," the farmer said.

Caleb patted him on the back, then they hopped in the truck and continued on their way. They stopped off at five more farms. At that point the pickup truck was so heavily loaded the suspension threatened to give way. Their last stop was Caleb's homestead where he ran in and retrieved his hunting rifle. As he climbed in the truck, he took one last look at Tabitha's cherry trees and smiled. "I'll either save your trees or I'll see you real soon," he said, bringing Tabitha's face to mind.

Bud turned onto the road and the truck trundled toward the village of Capulin. Just past the village, they turned on the highway that led to Folsom. There they saw Anderson along with a few other men parked by the side of the road. Bud pulled the truck to a stop and Caleb rolled down the window. Anderson stepped over and pointed up to the smoke billowing from the crater at the top of the mountain. "It's not going to be long now," he said. "I'd get out of here. I don't think you're going to stop it, no matter what you do."

"We've got to try," Caleb said.

"You don't even know the geologic structure of the area," Anderson argued. "You could blast out some rock and not weaken it enough to do any good at all."

In response, Bud cranked over the engine and Caleb rolled up the pick-up's window. They turned back onto the road. Looking behind, Caleb saw the scientists were busily packing up their gear, getting ready to get out of the area. Two more miles north, Bud pulled off the road and began rattling overland. Caleb was bounced around so much he hit his head on the ceiling of the truck. "Be careful there," he said. "You'll set off the dynamite!"

With that, Bud slowed down a little. "If we don't hurry, we may not have to worry about me setting off anything."

The sky started growing dark overhead, as though clouds were rolling in. Bud reached the base of the mountain and then drove up the gentle slope for a distance. Something bounced off the roof of the truck's cab. A few minutes later, something bounced off the hood. "Hail storm?" Caleb asked.

Bud shook his head. "No, I think it's some cinders from the volcano. We better stop here. It's now or never." He stopped the truck and the two men hopped out.

Caleb looked up at the sky. The horizons were the deep blue he'd grown used to in New Mexico, but overhead the smoke was growing black. Something like snow started falling from the smoke as they hauled the bags of fertilizer out of the truck bed. Caleb brushed one of them, leaving a dirty streak on his shirt. "Ash," he said.

"Yeah," Bud agreed. "The trees and brush up at the top must be getting pretty hot, starting to burn."

Without another word, the two men finished unloading the fertilizer. Caleb carefully set the dynamite on top of the bags. They both climbed back into the truck and Bud turned around and drove back off the mountain. A short distance away he stopped. "Okay, I think this should be safe."

They hopped out of the truck. Caleb raised the rifle and just as he was about to squeeze the trigger, the ground began shaking. He lowered the rifle.

"I think we better get out of here," Bud said, casting a nervous look at the darkening smoke from the top of the volcano.

"Just a few minutes more," Caleb said. "These tremors haven't been lasting long." He looked over at Bud who was shifting from one foot to the other. "Tell you what, you get in the truck and start her up."

The tremor died down and Bud nodded. "But I'm not leaving you behind."

"I don't want you to leave me behind," Caleb agreed. He waited until he heard the truck's engine roar to life, then he raised the rifle, took a deep breath, and squeezed the trigger. The first shot missed. He loaded another shell into the chamber, then fired again. The force of the blast knocked Caleb off his feet and everything went black.

He came to a few minutes later, feeling like he'd been thrown from a bull. Bud was on his knees shaking him. "We gotta get out of here, now," he said.

Caleb looked up and saw the fertilizer bomb they constructed had blown a sizable crater out of the side of the soft cinder cone. He stood up, brushing dirt and rubble from his clothes. Bud rushed around the other side, hopped in and closed the door. Just as Caleb hit the seat, Bud stomped on the accelerator and the truck shot forward, the passenger door closing on its own from the force of the acceleration.

"Do you think we did it?" Caleb asked.

Bud shook his head. "Who knows?" He looked over at his friend. "But you should have seen your face when that explosion knocked you on your butt." The two men laughed together as the truck reached the highway again and Bud pushed the accelerator to the floor. They rushed toward the northeast, away from the crater they'd dug.

Ten minutes later, just outside of Folsom, a tremendous explosion rocked the truck. Bud stomped on the brakes and the truck spun around on the dirt highway. When it stopped, they found themselves facing back toward Capulin. They saw a red plume going up into the sky—not from the crater at the top of the mountain, but near the hole they'd just dug. There was a geyser spouting molten rock, ash and cinders, but it was shooting to the northwest, away from all of the populated areas. "You did it!" Bud shouted, punching Caleb in the shoulder. "You saved the towns."

Caleb just shook his head while looking at the red plume of lava. It reminded him of a tree—the biggest cherry tree he had ever seen, covered with the brightest, most beautiful and vivid cherry blossoms he had ever seen. He looked over to Bud. "I think we did good, but let's get out of here. I think we're still a little close for comfort."

Mute, Bud just nodded, started the truck and turned around.

~ * ~

That night, Bud and Caleb arrived at Ethel and Glen's house in Raton. Caleb breathed a sigh of relief when he saw his old Model T parked out in front. As they climbed up the steps to the front door, it flew open, and Sherman ran out and hugged his father around the leg. Vinita stepped out and embraced her father. They turned around and looked back toward the East where the volcanic plume lit the night sky.

"I'm scared dad," Sherman said. "I'm scared for mom, all alone out by the volcano."

Caleb tousled his son's hair. "She's safe and so is the homestead and her trees. Who knows, maybe I'll even plant a few more....it seems fitting."

"I still think you should pack up," Bud said. "Get out of here and find some five-star hotel where you can be head chef."

Looking toward the house, Caleb saw Sherman Wallace standing in the door. He took a step forward and extended a hand toward his son-in-law. "I've been spending the afternoon talking to my grandson," he said. "I think today, I learned what a fine dad he has. I'm sorry for my words yesterday."

Caleb shook his hand. "I'm sorry Tab had to leave us both."

"She missed your finest hour, son," Wallace said.

Sherman looked back toward the glow in the east. "No, she had the best seat in the house."

Wallace and Caleb looked at each other and sighed. Without another word, they went inside and sat down to dinner. Even though Tabitha wasn't there, Caleb could feel her presence in the warmth of his son's smile and the wisdom of his father-in-law's words.

When dinner was finished, Caleb sat down on the front porch with Bud. "No, I don't think I'm quite ready to leave yet," he said. "I have to wait for fall. That's when the cherries will be ripe. Before I try cooking for those five-star restaurants, I better make sure I can make a good pie."

"I don't know if it's the smartest decision you've ever made, but I for one will be glad to have you around a little longer."

"Blasting a hole in the side of a volcano was probably not a smart decision, but I think it was the right one," Caleb said. "Hopefully this one will be, too. Besides, how many rodeos are there in cities with five-star restaurants? After all, I still have a score to settle with old Tornado."

"You don't think the rodeo is still on this weekend, do you?" Bud asked.

"I doubt it," Caleb said. "But, the volcano will die down and there will be another."

"I'm sure you're right," Bud said. He stood, patted his friend on the shoulder then went inside.

Caleb sat out on the porch and looked up at the stars, savoring life like he would savor a bittersweet cherry.

Cherry Blossoms in the Springtime first appeared in
This Ain't No Rodeo – WolfSinger Publications – 2008
Reprinted by permission of the author

~ * ~ * ~

David Lee Summers is the author of thirteen novels and one hundred short stories. His writing spans a wide range of the imaginative from science fiction to fantasy to horror. David's most recent works are *Ordeal of the Scarlet Order*, a novel of vampire mercenaries who fight evil, and *Breaking the Code*, a novella about a skinwalker preventing marines from recruiting Navajo Code Talkers at the beginning of World War II. His short stories have appeared in such magazines and anthologies as *Realms of Fantasy, Cemetery Dance,* and *Straight Outta Tombstone*. In addition to writing, David has edited five science fiction anthologies including *A Kepler's Dozen, Kepler's Cowboys* and *Maximum Velocity: The Best of the Full-Throttle Space Tales*. When not working with the written word, David operates telescopes at Kitt Peak National Observatory.

Learn more about David at http://www.davidleesummers.com

RIDE 'EM RAYMOND

Jean Martin

I suppose it was because we all grew up watching "Bonanza", "Gunsmoke" and "Rawhide", but as the seventies started winding down, there was a sudden craze for cowboys.

John Travolta, in those days strong, slender, and blessed with what my mother called bedroom eyes, played an urban cowpuncher, who swaggered through the city streets in boots and a Stetson, to ride a mechanical bull.

Dick Cavett interviewed some honest to goodness rodeo cowboys on his PBS talk show. Thousands of accountants, physio therapists and math teachers wore Stetsons and boots with their designer jeans.

Among these was Raymond Dodd. Ray was just out of MIT. He had a degree in computer science, and was in at the beginning of the high tech industry. So he made, for the time, pretty good money.

As a kid, he had decided, as some boys do, that he was Superman, James Bond and John Wayne all rolled into one. It never occurred to him only one of those three was real, and John Wayne was never a hero. He just played one.

He was a star on his junior high school football team, because he was three inches taller than any of his teammates. By high school, the other boys had caught up to him, so, while he was on the team, he spent most of his time on the bench.

But he ran track and won a couple of medals.

He played intramural football at MIT.

Out of college, he pumped iron and played handball at the gym.

In the summer, he played on a softball team called the Nads.

When mechanical bull riding became popular, he bought himself a Stetson hat, a pair of cowboy boots and learned to stay on a pseudo bovine.

His Stetson came from Brooks Brothers. But he'd ordered his boots from a company in Texas. In time, he bought some fancy belts with fancy buckles, that he wore with his designer jeans, when he went to The Gold Strike Saloon, over on South High Street.

The Gold Strike had a bar, kind of like the one in "Destry Rides Again".

Wanda Jakem, the hostess, dressed kind of like Miss Kitty in "Gunsmoke"

The waitresses all wore jeans that fit very well, cowboy shirts and boots.

The juke box played all the best country and western hits.

There was a mechanical bull.

You've seen one, maybe you've even ridden one, a leather covered rectangle, that spins around and bucks up and down, while somebody, who ought to know better, tries to stay on it.

Every second and fourth Saturday of the month, the Gold Strike Saloon sponsored a mechanical bull riding contest. The winner got a small trophy, a free drink and a kiss from Wanda Jakem.

Raymond had a collection of small trophies on the mantelpiece in his apartment.

When WYNN (Country in Columbus) sponsored a citywide mechanical bull riding championship at a Catholic school gym, Raymond took home the first-place trophy.

He put it in his front window, so the whole world, or at least anyone going down his street, could see it.

They had a picture of him over the bar at The Gold Strike Saloon holding his trophy and wearing his Brooks Brothers Stetson. Which meant a whole lot of hot shots came in to challenge him, lose and buy drinks.

Then WYNN (Country in Columbus) got a new manager, an ambitious young man with a lot of fresh ideas, some of which were actually good, but certainly not all of them.

The station sponsored a rodeo, every August, at a small arena, belonging to a small college just outside of town.

Families came out to see real, honest to goodness, cowboys and cowgirls, ride bucking broncos, race around barrels, bulldog steers, and, of course, ride bulls.

The new manager had, what he was certain, was a brilliant idea. That year's rodeo would include an amateur bull riding contest.

All those accountants and track coaches, who rode mechanical bulls in places like The Gold Strike Saloon, would have a chance to ride a real live bull, like real live rodeo cowboys.

The rodeo management wasn't thrilled with the idea. But the

prospect of increased ticket sales convinced them it wouldn't be too bad. The competitors would have to sign waivers, of course. The rodeo's lawyers, and the station's lawyers, insisted on that.

The rodeo found an elderly bull, that was used to being ridden. They thought he wouldn't be too dangerous.

They planned to have double the number of clowns on duty for the amateur contest.

WYNN (Country in Columbus) promoted their rodeo, complete with amateur bull riding competition, from Athens to Toledo.

Urban cowboys from all over the state signed up to ride a real, live bull.

Wanda Jakem, herself, presented Raymond with a copy of the entry form and waiver, at his table at the Gold Strike Saloon.

Raymond was eager, until he saw the waiver, absolving WYNN and the rodeo promoters of any liability should he be injured trying to ride an aggressive animal that resented having people on its back.

It wasn't until after he'd had two successful rides on the mechanical bull, and a tequila sunrise, that he filled out the form and signed the waiver, as his many admirers cheered.

It meant the Gold Strike Saloon promoted the rodeo, and most of the regulars bought tickets, and planned to go.

That Sunday afternoon, they all headed for the arena, including Raymond Dodd, wearing his Brooks Brothers Stetson, his designer jeans, his real cowboy boots and carrying a thermos full of tequila sunrise.

He swaggered through the other urban cowboys, tipping his hat to the pretty ladies, generally acting like he was auditioning for the part of Wyatt Earp.

Then he saw the bull.

The mechanical bull made a whirring noise, like a machine, as it bucked and turned.

The actual bull snorted and snarled.

The mechanical bull had no head, and no horns.

The actual bull had horns which he thought looked very long and sharp.

The actual bull was confined to a pen, and did not look happy to be there. It looked like it wanted to get out and hurt somebody.

More to the point, it was able to buck the first contestant off in two point nine seconds. Having done so, it chased him around the arena until the clowns convinced it to chase them instead.

Several mechanical bull riders resigned from the competition.

Raymond reached for his thermos. He thought of his trophies and his friends at the Gold Strike.

He wasn't obviously drunk when he climbed onto the bull, or he wouldn't have been allowed to compete.

But, as he swung his leg over, one of the actual cowboys thought he smelled liquor, and asked him, "Are you sure you want to do this?"

Raymond handed him his Brooks Brothers Stetson and said yes.

The mechanical bull bucked and turned, but it stayed in one place. The actual bull galloped across the arena, doing whatever it could to get this annoying human off its back. While doing so, it snorted, bellowed and made other intimidating noises.

Raymond managed to hang on for almost two seconds, before the actual bull shook him off.

He was smart enough to roll away, avoiding the flying hooves. Then he jumped up and ran like Hell for the fence.

Perhaps the bull resented him a little bit more than the other competitors, because it chased him across the arena. It managed to hook one of its horns in his designer jeans, and tear off most of the seat, as Raymond was climbing a fence.

Rodeo fans got to enjoy the sight of his lucky boxers, bright green, decorated with yellow horseshoes, as he fled to safety.

Raymond Dodd left his Stetson at the rodeo. He was never seen again at the Gold Strike Saloon, even though they kept his picture over the bar, along with a picture of him fleeing the rodeo arena in his torn pants.

He gave his real cowboy boots and fancy belts to an Episcopal church rummage sale.

He had, he would tell his friends, lost interest in bull riding. He wanted to serve his country.

As the eighties progressed, there were new heroes on the screen, military men replaced cowboys.

Sylvester Stallone was Rambo. Tom Cruise was Top Gun.

Raymond enlisted in the National Guard.

They were eager to have him, because of his computer skills. He would have a long and successful career as a weekend warrior.

He never saw any actual combat, but he did get to wear a real uniform. He was even deployed to Saudi Arabia during Desert Storm.

When he came home, he was in a parade down South High Street. He rode in a Humvee, right past where the Gold Strike Saloon used to be, before it closed during the recession, in 1990.

Some boys decide they are Superman, James Bond and John Wayne all rolled into one.

Most of them outgrow the idea. Some of them have to learn the hard way they aren't their movie heroes.

Raymond Dodd was one of those boys.

Learning can cost them dearly.

Happily it cost Raymond no more than his dignity, his Brooks Brothers Stetson and a pair of designer jeans.

Jean Martin has a BS degree in Journalism from Ohio University and has been laughing about it for longer than she cares to admit. She lives, at present, in McKeesport, Pennsylvania, with an orange tabby cat named Samwise, who likes bagpipe music.

STEER MAGIC

Kit Muse

Harrel backed his big sorrel mare, Doc's Sunset Lady, into the box. This rodeo between Springfield, MO and Oklahoma City was too small to have a proper chute and barrier, but he didn't have to worry about Lady jumping too soon. In spite of the threat of Prohibition spirits were high and no doubt flowing among the crowd. They cheered at his name; he was relatively well-known, as was the big red mare with the flaxen mane and tail he rode. Lady read steer better than he did, and that said something considering he was the one who flung himself from her back to wrestle the creature to the ground.

The guys said this one likes to wobble off the line a bit. He told his *socius*, or bonded magical companion. No magic in mundane rodeos; that was the rule he ran by. Other cowboys weren't so ethical, but he'd still beat them fair and square. He preferred it that way. Made the bragging that much better and the beer all the colder.

I know. He's trying to hide his thoughts, but he's running to the right. Be ready! Lady said, and a few moments later, the flag dropped, the man released the steer and it bolted—directly to the right.

It was a runner too, and they were nearly halfway down the arena before Lady pulled up alongside. He judged his distance, leaned out of his saddle, and jumped, wrapping his arms around the steer's horns and drawing it to the ground. A swift swipe of his legs sent the steer onto his side, all four feet in the air, and the referee dropped the flag, his round over.

"Damn, that was good," the pickup man said as he brought Lady back to Harrel. "Glad I didn't bet against ya."

"Thanks. Though Lady does all the work." He put his foot in the stirrup and swung into the saddle, then waved his hat at the cheering crowd. His time was good, damn good for such an onery steer, and he hoped he remained at the top. The prize money would give him enough for dinner and gas to get to the next rodeo.

He rode out of the arena thinking he hadn't always run so thin in the wallet. Lady and he worked well together, and usually made enough on the circuit they didn't have to worry about the off season. He wasn't exactly pro, but he also didn't need to hold down another job. Except now it was looking as if he might have to.

He stayed close to the gate, hearing the time for the rider after him announced. He remained in the lead. The last few guys could beat him, if they were having a good day, and most of the time it wasn't a good day for them.

The tingle of magic made the hair on the back of his neck rise. This was a mundane event, no mages here. At least not many and they tended to stick together. He knew of a pair who participated in team roping, but they, like he, tried to win on their own merits, not magical powers. A couple of cowboys he knew used a bit of power to stick to a bronc or bull, but usually only made it appear like a magical ride. This was different.

This also could be the reason why he hadn't been placing as high as he usually did. He watched the cowboy back into the box on a horse one of the guys let other riders use. It wasn't magical. No *socius* he knew would allow multiple riders on its back. Harrel focused his magical sight on the rider. The saddle glowed, the tell-tale sign someone wanted to cheat.

Normally he'd blame the cowboy, but this one didn't have a lick of magic in him. No, if he had to place bets, Harrel would have said the magic came from the owner of the horse, and though he'd seen this one a few times now in this round, he didn't know the owner. In fact, he would have bet he'd never seen the big bay horse with three white socks and a strip of white down its face before.

He tried to trace the magic back to its source, but then the man dropped the flag and the other released the steer and the rider took off. This steer veered to the left, getting almost too close to the cowboy, but he nudged the horse to the left, then made his move. A solid catch brought the steer to the ground, but his legs hung up underneath him. The man did everything he could, but the steer folded in on itself and would not budge.

A push of magic strong enough to ruffle Harrel's hair rushed past him, and then the steer lay flat. The flag dropped and the time was announced. It put him in second place. The cowboy left the arena with a smile after retrieving the horse.

"Damn good time considering what happened," the cowboy leaning on the fence said.

Harrel nodded. "Yep," he agreed. "You wouldn't know who owns that horse, would you?"

"That's Zebidiah Overton's horse." The cowboy spat tobacco, then jerked his chin up toward the fancy box next to the stands. "He doesn't ride anymore, but that horse is out of his best stud. Heard he refused a lot of money for that horse."

"Well, I've refused a lot of money for mine, too," Harrel replied.

"Won Calgary on it last year. Then something happened and he stopped riding," the cowboy continued.

That was where he'd heard the name before. He'd ridden against Zebediah a few times, mostly beat him. His horse might be good, but he didn't have the connection with it that he had with Lady. Considering the bond between horse and rider, he didn't figure a little direct communication was cheating. He still needed to grab the steer by the horns and flip him with the fastest time, and that was all him. "I was there," Harrel replied. "Beat me by half a second."

"Damn shame he isn't riding anymore."

Another rider went, missing his steer.

"Well, looks like you won this one. Congrats," the cowboy said. Then with a touch of his hat, he turned and walked away. If Harrel thought he sensed malice in the words, it was only a feeling because the man had acted cordial enough.

Sure enough a few minutes later the placings were announced and he mounted Lady and galloped into the arena, his hat held high. He made the circuit of the arena and left, taking Lady back to her stall.

"You had a good ride," a gravelly voice said in the barn aisle. "Almost too good."

Harrel straightened from picking out Lady's feet and turned toward the voice. A tall man, thin and wiry as if an illness had sucked the vitality out of him. His black cowboy hat sat low on his head and a long gray duster covered him down to his boots. "A good horse makes all the difference," he said. "Harrel Konnor. And you might be?"

"Zebediah Overton. I watched your run. Nearly flawless."

Harrel didn't like the way Zebediah looked at him or the way the man was looking at Lady. He stepped out of the stall and shut the door behind him, making sure to keep the latch behind his back, just in case. "Lots of practice. You won Cheyenne last year, so you ought to know." There, let him put that in his pipe and smoke it. Harrel knew who he was. "Come just to tell me I rode well, which the pay-out will also tell me, or did you want something?" He dared not reach out with his magical senses, but something about Zebediah was off. Like the man dabbled in things that ought to lay buried.

"And you came in second there. I've had my eye on you for a long time, Harrel Konnor. You and Lady. You were doing this before the war wasn't you?"

"We were."

"Then maybe it's about time Lady retired and started making colts. Don't you think? Sure would be a shame to have her talent go to waste."

Bet he thought that was the job of all women, Harrel thought to himself. "Lady will tell me when it's time. Not time yet."

"And if I make you an offer you can't refuse?"

Harrel smiled slowly. "I can refuse a great many things, Zebediah Overton, and an offer from you would be among them. I wish you good day." He tipped his hat toward the man, letting him know there'd be no hard feelings if he left. He'd come, made his offer, and been refused. Leaving would be the gentlemanly thing to do at this point, but he suspected Zebediah wasn't a gentleman.

"I suspected you'd say that, but I had to try anyway." He turned on his heel and walked down the aisle toward the stands. The next event had started.

All Harrel wanted to do was pick up his check, load Lady in his trailer, and get on the road. The sooner he was out of here and away from that man, the better they'd both be. He glanced down the aisle and saw Bobby, a calf roper walking his way.

"Hey, you doing anything at the moment?" he asked Bobby.

The young man shook his head, blond strands visible below his tan cowboy hat. "Was just comin' to see if you wanted me to watch your stall while you collected your check?" He grinned, showing a few missing teeth. "You were like lightning out there today." He glanced over his shoulder. "That Zebediah wishes he rode as well as you. His horse is good 'nuf, but not as good as you and Lady together."

"Thanks. I appreciate that. You headed over to Amarillo?"

"Yeah, me n' Joe are leaving tomorrow morning. Probably stop-ping at home for a few days. Hey, want to stay a day or two? Can't miss Joe's wife's cookin'. The baby's nearly a year old, so it's not so bad, but the weather will be warm enough to sleep in your truck if you want."

"Thanks. I'll think about it. Wasn't sure what I was going to do for a few days." Staying with Joe and his growing family would help his money last. "I've got hay and feed if I do, so won't put you out."

"You're a good one, Harrel. Go get your check. You earned it." He clapped Harrel on the shoulder as he walked past.

Relieved Bobby would be keeping an eye on Lady, no doubt while Joe did the same over their two horses and gear, he hurried to the rodeo office.

"Hey, Harrel," the white-haired man who had always run the rodeo office said. He spat tobacco juice into a can and thumbed through the ledger in front of him. "Got your money right here. Give me a sec'."

"Take your time, Doc." Whether he'd been a doctor or not, Harrel didn't know, and probably no one else knew either. Everyone called him Doc. "I know you're on top of things. Always are."

"Entries down a bit. Still recovering after the war. And those damn Prohibitionists aren't helping. How can a man enjoy some cowboyin' if he doesn't have a beer in his hand." Doc spat tobacco juice again. "Zeb will be in soon to get his money. Always has me split them between him and the guys who rent his horse." Doc shook his head. "Damn man shouldn't rent out his horse if he can't trust a man to pay him. But without him we wouldn't have the entries we do. He'll be disappointed one of his riders didn't win."

Disappointed was a mild way to put it, Harrel thought. He accepted the money and put it in his wallet. "Thank you, kindly."

"If you're headed out tonight and want to go as far as Oklahoma City, you can stop at Dott's Motel. Tell her I sent you and she'll treat you right."

"Thanks. Not sure of my plans yet." He didn't like to advertise his plans. With a tip of his hat to Doc, he turned and left the cramped show office. He made his way to the barn area, passing a storage area.

Magic wrapped around him, hauling him against the wooden wall hard enough to make it rattle.

"What the—?" Harrel lifted his hands and thrust them against the energy holding him tight.

He muttered a few words of a releasing spell his grandma had taught him, and the magic eased. He turned, firing an offensive spell he'd learned on his own, not enough to hurt his attacker, but it'd sting and make sure whoever it was—and Harrel had a good idea—knew he wasn't unarmed. Stepping into the center of the walkway he turned to face the darkened corridor between this storage area and the main barns. "Show yourself," he called.

Zebediah Overton moved from the shadow, almost as if he had to separate himself from it. Harrel hadn't learned enough about the different types of magic to be able to identify it, but it certainly came from the less ethical side of the magical line. "Heard Doc telling you about Dott's place in Oklahoma City. I suggest you turn around and try a rodeo somewhere else. I hear there might be one by Raleigh next weekend."

Even if he had gas money to make it to Raleigh doing so held little appeal. "Why? And leave all the fun of Amarillo to you?"

"Amarillo and the rodeos that come after, yeah. This is my circuit. Me and my boys, we do okay."

"And if I don't?" He knew the answer to that question. His momma didn't raise no fool; he knew the reason why she'd left him with his grandmother and ran off leaving him behind. She hadn't loved his daddy, and frankly, neither had he. But he'd dealt with mean bastards before, and Zebediah didn't scare him. His magic had come in the night his father had visited him, and through his partially open bedroom door, he'd watched his father smack the only person who'd cared for him. Rage and magic poured through him, and before he knew it, his father had slammed against the opposite wall, knocked out cold.

Harrel shrugged off the memory. The cold hand of magic wrapped itself around his throat, squeezing hard enough to make it difficult to breathe. *Oh hell no.* He focused his magic like a trick rider's whip, slinging it at Zebediah.

The magic hit him, making his eyes going wide and his concentration slip just enough the magic around his throat eased.

Harrel rushed forward. Never use magic when fists would do, he'd learned, and his magic dueling skills were rusty at best. His shoulder caught Zebediah in the center of his chest, sending him sprawling backwards against the boards. For a moment it was his father laying sprawled there, though Zebediah wasn't unconscious. He moved, another magic attack, no doubt. Men like him didn't like to get their hands dirty.

Pausing long enough to throw up shields, he dove for Zebediah, landing a powerful right cross with the same strength he'd use to flip a steer. Blood trickled from a cut lip and a second punch bloodied his nose.

"You bastard!" Zebediah called. "You could have had it all. Just sell your mare and—"

"Never!" Harrel snarled as he landed another blow. A rib cracked under the impact, and Zebediah snarled. "All I want to do is ride and flip steers. I don't know what the hell you want, but you attacked me. Remember? A gentleman accepts no for an answer." Another blow, and then another, until Zebediah lay against the wooden wall, his chin on his chest.

"You'll regret this."

"Maybe I will. Maybe I won't." He stepped back, straightened, and tossed a binding spell on the man. It'd keep him down for at least a couple of hours. Long enough for him to get cleaned up and head out of town. Bobby's offer sounded nice, but he wouldn't bring this kind of storm down on them. After all, Oklahoma City wasn't the only rodeo he could attend, and he did his best thinking on the road.

Harrel strode back to the stall, pausing at a hydrant to wash the blood off his knuckles. No one saw him, and when he returned to find Bobby sitting in front of his stall, he thanked him for being so vigilant.

"Will we see you at Joe's place?" Bobby asked as he headed back to his stalls.

"Let me think about it. I'm itching for a change of scenery," he said. Knowing Zeb probably had ears most places, he figured someone would overhear Bobby and Joe talking and it'd get back to him.

"Safe travels. Hope we cross paths again soon." Bobby nodded, then turned on his heel and left.

"Oh we will," Harrel said as he stepped into Lady's stall and ran his hand down her shoulder. *How would you fancy a trip to Oklahoma City?*

And miss the fun? Laugher filled Lady's mental voice. *I trust you have a plan for dealing with Zebediah?*

You know I do. After all, the only magic we need is a strong arm and a good horse. I'm lucky I have both. He checked the saddle girth and hooked his bridle over the saddle horn. The rest of Lady's gear was in his truck, locked and warded, so all he needed to do was to load Lady in the trailer. Then, he'd be on the road. He always did his best thinking when he drove, and soon enough, he'd be in Oklahoma City just in time to work a little steer magic. Somehow, he didn't think running into Zebediah would be a problem.

~ * ~ * ~

For **Kit Muse** storytelling is everything, and there's never been a time when they weren't creative. Kit writes fantasy set in her *Musimagium* world featuring animal companions, many of them horses, magic and music. In addition, they write equestrian literature.

They live on a homestead in the Ozarks with a sacred herd of rescue horses. Sharing the homestead with Kit and the horses are their spouse, a flock of chickens, and many cats.

They've been writing professionally since 2002 and have written in multiple genres under multiple pen names. When not writing or working on the homestead, they enjoy playing the clarinet, researching ancient religions, listening to podcasts, and reading/watching/consuming speculative fiction media. They're currently a graduate student pursuing a MA in Religious Studies.

Pronouns: they/them
Website: https://KitAuthor.com

It's a Family Thing

Kathy Roberts

The American cowboy is surely brother to the European Knight, who helps damsels in distress, rights wrongs and is loyal and brave.

Well, okay. Maybe the Cowboy Ethic is not quite the Code of Chivalry, but loyalty, a good work ethic, and a sense that when one word will do why spend time and energy on twenty, has to rank up there pretty high. A cowboy (and when I say cowboy, I am including cowgirls) is honest, to a fault sometimes, and he is tough, but fair.

I have always loved and been in awe of cowboys, after all, they are the heroes of the West. I ditched a college English major (much to my Mother's chagrin) in favor of an agriculture major because the life style appealed to me. I could see myself riding, roping, running barrels and throwing bales of hay around. At the time, I rode hunter /jumpers, but that didn't feel important. It was dallying and sorting cows that seemed to count for me. I yearned for a life full of cows, horses, ranches and blue skies.

It was no surprise I met my future husband at Cal Poly, SLO. I picked him out of the herd of cowboys that included cattlemen, and ranchers, future world Champion Larry Ferguson, and Lee Rosser of the famous Cotton Rosser family.

My new husband was a team roper, and I couldn't wait to learn how to throw a rope and chase a steer down the pen. Rope management wasn't quite as easy as I had thought it would be, but I was determined. I was going to be a heeler, since it seemed there were way too many things to consider as a header. You first had to watch the steer and call for it at precisely the right time, then you had to make sure you rode the barrier correctly. Then, you had to catch the cow, rate it, and then throw and make that perfect horn catch. But additionally, you had to dally (carefully, so not to lose fingers) turn the steer, provide a great handle for your heeler and then, know exactly the right moment to turn and face up. The timing had to be perfect as you held your dally until the flagger dropped the flag.

It just seemed like a lot to do compared to the heeler, who came out of the box, rode to his position, made the corner, threw the perfect heel loop, dallied and then stopped. It appeared to be a no-brainer to me.

Of course, once I began to actually throw the rope, (I was left-handed, and learning to rope right-handed) I realized there was a lot more to heeling than I thought. Rope management was only the beginning. The perfect heel loop was a lot more difficult than the perfect head loop, but I practiced and practiced. And, after several years of totally spastic loops, I was fairly good.

We team roped for almost twenty years in California. We enjoyed trying to become better ropers and worked at becoming better horsemen, but the best thing about roping was the camaraderie. Cowboys and rodeo families in particular feel like part of a huge family of people who live the Western life no matter where they live. As soon as a person joins this family, they are welcomed as if they had been born into it. Everyone roots for the next person in the box, everyone cheers when they win, and everyone will help out with suggestions if a roper hits a dry spot. Myself, I hit many dry spots; there were weekends I never caught anything, followed by a weekend in which I couldn't miss. Who knew you had to be lucky as well as good to win.

When I was pretty new at roping, my husband and I attended the American Cowboy Team Roping Association, ACTRA, finals in Tulare. As I backed into the heeler's box, I was nervous. I didn't know whether to hope he caught or not. If he missed I looked pretty good riding down to the catch pen; if he caught, it was up to me to finish the job. We were roping in the number four roping, in the afternoon heat and dust. He not only caught, but turned three perfect steers for me. They were in the same place in the arena and he handled them just about as good as could ever be. It was like following the Heel-o-matic.

I think I held my breath until the flag was down, and I was amazed he dragged all three steers into my loop and all three were clean. Whoops and cheers came from friends and strangers alike who watched.

It was then the real tension began.

We made the finals.

I worried all the way until we rode into the boxes at about one thirty AM. I prayed I could catch my fourth steer. My husband nodded. The steer left and a second later, my husband's horse followed.

All I could think of was 'don't be late' as I urged my grey horse out of the box. It was just like the three times before; the same spot, the same Heel-o-matic shot. When it was all over and we headed for the catch pen, I think I was oblivious to anything that happened in the last minute. I had caught, and caught clean. I didn't even hear the applause and cheers this time, but we came in third, and we ended up third.

I was ecstatic.

For the next several weeks, people I knew and people I hardly knew sent congratulations. They were excited because we had won as a couple when at the time, there weren't a lot of husband and wife teams. It was the first time I really understood what it was to be part of the team roping family. So many people were genuinely happy for us and for our accomplishment.

Many times, and with many of the same ropers, on weekends or at larger ropings, we hauled living quarters trailers of some kind . We camped out and after the ropings, gathered for a potluck. Some dishes were cooked the cowboy way in Dutch ovens, some on a BBQ grill, but I ate some of the best foods I ever tasted. Perhaps it was the company, perhaps it was the talented cooks, perhaps it was both.

In the winter, we journeyed to Arizona for several weeks and some of the best times I can remember were those where we roped in the mornings and then, the "girls" all went shopping in and around Phoenix. The dinner fare was normally planned out and one of the roper's dads (who didn't rope, but who enjoyed engineering meals for all of us) assigned jobs so the meal was not all one person's responsibility. There wasn't much that could have compared to those trips to Arizona.

My Mother, who was raised on a sheep ranch in South Dakota, enjoyed hearing about my roping adventures and was a huge sup-porter of me and almost everything I did. But, pretty much in the middle of my roping career, she was diagnosed with Dementia. When my roping family heard about her affliction, I heard stories of how many of them had been dealing with dementia and suddenly, we had another thing in common. As time progressed, so did the disease and my role changed from child to parent. It was difficult to watch a woman who had been a computer programmer and who successfully played the stock market on her own, have trouble with numbers. She knew what was happening and it made her angry and resentful. Over three years, I watched my Mother slowly disappear.

The last year of her life was the worst. She fell and broke her ankle. She would call me several times in an hour; one time she was angry, another call was hysterical, and yet another would be confused, asking about how her parents were.

I was desperate for relief. I needed a way to get a break from the mental strain of dealing with dementia. I asked my husband if we could rope enough to try and win a year-end saddle, and thankfully, he agreed. I don't know what I would have done had it not been for my roping "family". I needed the distraction, I needed the occasional success, and I needed to be around people who were supportive.

We attended over one hundred and thirty ropings that year. There were six divisions in the ACTRA year end program. I got to know the five or six of us in my District who were running for the saddles better than I ever thought I would. We were hunting points and even though we had to work early the next morning, we were there, together, for the fifty points we got just to show up, and hoping to place in the jackpot to add a few more.

For an hour or two, or three, I got that mental break I so desperately needed. I am a low numbered roper, who learned to concentrate on the job of catching those crafty cows, who got a little better at heeling, because I could escape into a friendly world where little mattered except the clock and honing my skills. I could go to my Mother's side refreshed and able to help her; I was more patient and the understanding of my friends helped me be more understanding with her.

I had settled into a fairly comfortable spot in my life when my heeling horse developed white line disease and lost most of the outer shell of his left front foot. It was severe blow to my plans to win the saddle and to maintain my sanity. When the roping community heard about my horse, I had offers from multiple people, some of whom were roping against me for the saddle in my division, to loan me a horse. The outpouring of consideration was truly awesome and inspiring. I began to see life was complicated; people were complicated.

My saving grace was that one of my husband's heading horses had been a pretty good heeling horse. He wasn't my gray horse, but he was a great substitute in a pinch. I continued to rope. I dropped out of the lead a time or two, but then caught back up.

We had a little over two months until the end of our roping year when I started getting little headaches. I attributed them to stress, but they continued to get worse and worse. I went to the doctor and he gave me pills that didn't work. Over and over, we tried different medications, but the headaches only got worse. After a month, they were so bad I could hardly stand to walk around. They were a little better if I lay down, but nothing seemed to work.

Between trying to see Mother and still trying to maintain my lead in the standings, and the pain, I began to realize I couldn't live this way. I called to see the doctor and asked to be seen that day. My regular doctor wasn't there and the one I saw thankfully sent me to a Neurologist the next day.

He asked if I had been bucked off recently. I said no. Had I been in a car accident recently? No. Had I had any medical procedures recently? Again no.

He nodded his head and said he was pretty sure he knew what was wrong, but a test would tell for sure.

The results were in. I had a hole in my spinal column and the cerebral fluid was draining out. Effectively, I was a quart low on oil. The answer was a blood patch in which my own blood was drawn then injected into my spinal column. The injection would both bring the level up and provide a clot which would stop the leakage.

I was skeptical, but at this point it was either get better or put me down. Two hours later, I had the injection and spent an hour and a half, face down, upside down, encouraging a clot to develop.

When I finally got up it was amazing. My headache was nearly gone and I was ecstatic. The bad news was that for the next eight weeks, I was not to ride, run, jump or lift anything heavier than five pounds. Five pounds is not that much. A good pair of boots and a belt buckle almost weigh that much.

I had to wear soft soled shoes because the jarring of a hard sole might loosen the clot. I was probably the only person in California who desperately wanted a blood clot.

With about month left, I resigned myself to the fact I probably wouldn't win the saddle. It wasn't as hard a pill to swallow as I thought it might be since I was finally free from those excruciating headaches.

About that time, the older gentleman who was in second place came up to me at a roping. He said he'd heard about my medical issues. His wife had been bugging him to travel with her, so he was going to take the next month off. There was no one who could have caught either of us, and I told him he didn't have to do that. His answer was yes, he did; his wife would kill him if he didn't. He winked at me and we both knew she wouldn't have killed him, but I can tell you that right then, I knew what a blessing our roping friends were.

The saddle wasn't the big deal. It was the friendships and the good will, respect and the relationships borne of cows, horses, cowboys and cowgirls mixed in with a lot of dirt and cemented by sweat and try.

In September, I won the saddle in my division, as did the six other ropers who had been with me, shivering in Penn Valley on a Wednesday night as snow covered the trucks and trailers in twenty-eight-degree weather.

We all hugged each other knowing how each one of us had triumphed and that team roping had done a spectacular thing for us. The competition spurred us on, the camaraderie strengthened us when we thought we might give up.

The beginning of November, my Mother passed away. I was thankful she was finally at peace. There is always a hole left when a loved one dies, but I rested, certain I had done what was needed.

That was also a year of discovery.

That was a year of ups and downs, of trials and tribulations, but it was also a year of friendship and love and understanding. It was the year my husband stood by me in every way, and it was one of many years that my rodeo family had my back and supported me.

I will always remember that year as the worst year of my life as well as the best year of my life.

This is the story of life, not only my life, but life as a whole. There will always be good things that happen as well as bad things. The source of the courage to face life, is friends and family. Without people around us whom we can rely upon we cannot succeed and be truly happy. I am happy with my own family but until I made room for my rodeo family, I didn't realize family is not a blood thing, it is a loving thing.

Life is fragile and the only way to strengthen each and every life is to rely on friends and family. It's surely that way with team roping —you have to rely on and trust your partners. The feeling of that perfect catch is what makes us all try again and what allows us to live life to the fullest.

~ * ~ * ~

Kathryn Roberts lives in California with her husband of over 50 years. Five horses, four cows and five dogs complete a family worthy of hours and hours of attention.

Born in South Dakota, she moved to Seattle, San Francisco and Tracy, California with her family and when she landed at Cal Poly, San Luis Obispo, she met Elliott, her future husband. After getting married, they had a son, and ended up settling in Granite Bay, near Sacramento where they owned and operated a business for over thirty years. She was active in the Chamber of Commerce and 4-H, as well as a member of Placer County's Mounted Search and Rescue Unit.

Retirement brought more time for roping, sorting, and trialing working cattle dogs. They spent nearly ten years supporting California High School Rodeo and she was the State Queen coordinator.

Writing is relaxing for her, and she is the author of three non-fiction books as well as several romance novels, with, of course, cowboy heroes and cowgirl heroines.

THIRTY SECONDS

Sara Brett

Geez Louise's muscles tremble as I hold her back in the alley waiting my turn. I feel her hot breath blowing against my knee as she turns to itch her nose. I let her have head space before an event, just a little bit, to keep her calm. Talk about calm. I'm not calm but I'm good at pretending. I'm so keyed up I'm surprised she's not snorting, ready to take us through our paces. I'm surprised I can hold her here. Waiting. Still as quivering muscles can be.

She's not the horse I was promised. I was promised a Quarter Horse, was working towards purchasing a Quarter Horse. I had been at the birth of said Quarter Horse, watched the birth sack break open and the foal tumble out. I touched him, and sang to him and backed away to give his mother room. Sid, the rancher, smiled at me; he knew the foal was mine.

But like turning on a dime, making a perfect run doesn't always turn out the way you planned.

I spent afternoons after school having the colt bond with me, follow me, fed him sweet molasses nuggets, sang him cowboy songs —he liked the Roy Rogers theme song, Happy Trails, the best, and the Bonanza theme my father had taught me. I cleaned stalls, chipping away at my bill.

My father was putting up half the cost.

His rodeo days were behind him, his back, his neck, and his knees wouldn't let him take the brunt of falling. Truth be told, he couldn't take the brunt of my mom being so mad at him when he got hurt, which was, to her mind, always. I'm twelve, too young to know so much, I know, but barrel racers start young. You have to start young to have the required lightning reflexes to fall right. I've been riding all my life, since before I was born, since my mom rode in the saddle, carrying me in utero.

~ * ~

I came home from the stable next door to our farm, walked in the front door, ready to set my hat on the rack, and right in front of me, my father fell down the stairs, reaching out to catch himself, dislocating his left arm. He got up as though he was mostly okay, holding his left wrist in his right hand.

"Shells, you know what to do," he turned his left shoulder towards me, waiting for me to grab hold of his wrist, and lift his arm and wrist simultaneously, setting his dislocated arm back into its socket. You got to do it fast, before the swelling starts, while the adrenaline blocks the pain. He fell so many times, reaching out with his arm to block his falls that later, it dislocated randomly and far too often. He never took the time for it to heal in between, let the ligaments chill out; he had too much work to do, too many rides. It's true, what doctors said—once dislocated, bound to happen again. My mom and I both knew the drill. So, I grasped his wrist and his upper arm then lifted them up, bent at the elbow, until his upper arm and wrist were level with his collar bone and held them steady, waiting for the click. The Saint Sebastian medal he wears around his neck on a chain twinkles, catching the light. This time it really seemed to hurt him more than other times, he was sweating and turning gray. "I'm going fast as I can Dad, but you've told me to go steady, I can't move it any faster or it won't drop in."

Nobody talks about how heavy the dislocated arm is as you lift it. Then, it clicked, loudly, and I pushed back slightly to ease it the rest of the way, and the weight is gone, my signal to ease the wrist and arm down.

He held his arm to his side, "Good job," he said, and promptly fell on the floor. On his bad arm.

"Dad." I didn't shake him, didn't want to jolt his just-set arm. But, he shouldn't be lying on it either.

"Mom," I yelled, then grabbed the landline and dialed 911.

"This line is being recorded. What's your emergency?"

"Something's wrong with my Dad, he dislocated his arm, we got it back in, but then he fell, he's all gray, and sweaty. He won't answer me."

They got our address, asked about my mom, but I didn't know where she was, she could be anywhere, out in the garden, visiting her sister, riding her own horse. We have poor or non-existent cell phone service and internet, so, few people carry a cell phone.

The ambulance came, my mom still at random. They placed big ping pong paddles on him and shocked him, but he doesn't look any better. They put small white pills under his tongue, set him on a stretcher, slid him into the ambulance then put a needle with a tube attached into his arm.

"I'm riding with him," I insisted, my white cowboy hat still on my head.

"It has to be an adult."

"I'm twelve. He's my Dad. He's not riding alone."

"Alright, but stay out of the way."

I sat by him, holding his fingers because his arm had the IV in it. "That shoulder was just dislocated. Be careful," I told them.

The sirens blared the whole way.

At the emergency room, they wouldn't let me go any further. A nurse tried calling my mother. I sat in a hard orange plastic chair.

"Code Blue, Code Blue," echoed through the halls.

A tall, thin doctor rushed out, looking for my mother. "She's not here yet," I said. "She doesn't even know he's here. What's wrong with him?"

"Let's wait for your mother."

"I know what Code Blue means. It was for him, wasn't it?"

"Let's wait…" he started, but I ran past him, down the hall to the right, and there was my father, lying still on a gurney with tubes on him the nurses were taking out.

"Dad." I lay my head on his right shoulder, his shirt still holding the circular leads from what I later learned was an ECG machine.

"You can't be here." A nurse reached for me to escort me out.

The doctor, right behind me, said, "Let her have a minute, her father just died."

I lifted my head. "Did I do it? Did I set his arm wrong? He fell down the stairs, and it dislocated."

The doctor crouched down before me. "He fell down the stairs? And dislocated his arm?"

I nodded yes. "I reset it. I've done it before."

"What your father had was a heart attack. It might be why he fell down the stairs. You did nothing to cause this. From his records, he already had significant heart trouble. He was lucky to have you with him. By calling the ambulance so quickly you gave him a second chance, all the chances he could have. But I'm afraid you'll have to go back out into the hall till an adult comes. You're a minor. Regulations. Come on." He led me back out. "Good job," he said leaving me, just the way my father said it. "Good job."

~ * ~

After they found my mother, but before the funeral, the lawyer told us what my mother didn't know. She was going to lose the farm. There wasn't enough money coming in. Same old story I'd heard all my life but this time it had an ending. Farmers always juggle money, the same way they juggle the weather. They ride with it.

My father had let his life insurance policy lapse. My mother swallowed that, and I didn't really understand what that meant. She could try to keep his truck rental business going, but there wasn't enough money coming in to pay more than two more mortgage payments, not to mention the quarterly tax bills. I knew all about those because I picked up the mail from the end of our mile-long driveway and carried the bills to the house when I returned from school or Sid's ranch.

The farm was mortgaged, which my mother knew, to get the truck business going since my father quit riding bulls, and people didn't have enough money to rent stalls for horses anymore, which they had managed together.

She could make one of the truck drivers the manager and try to make that work.

Farmers do not get social security unless they pay into it on their own or a pension plan unless they create some form of plan and pay into that. To cover that, there was the life insurance policy which no one likes to talk about and which no longer existed. Apparently, my mother had been counting on the life insurance as a buffer.

And there was not enough money coming from anywhere anymore, without my Dad, to pay for my horse no matter how many stalls I cleaned.

I had spent as much time as I could after school working my colt, brushing his short caramel coat. Because of his low wicker and how he leaned forward stretching his two front legs to eat, as all colts do, I named him Wicket. He was following me without a bridle or lead-rope as I had taught him when Sid walked over to me.

He took his cigarette out of his mouth, I'll say that for him, and talked while waving it in the air like he was signing documents in smoke. "Your Dad and I had a deal. That colt is worth twenty-five thousand dollars easy. He was good for it, working it off in free truck trailering, installments, truck repair, and other things. I don't see it happening now. I'm sorry, Shelby But, I have an immediate buyer. I appreciate the time you put into gentling him, and I figure I owe you two thousand for your efforts and time, as it made the colt worth more. Do we have a deal?"

I held out my hand, then heard my dad say, clear as a bell, "Let's talk it over with your mother."

I was so surprised I dropped my outstretched hand.

"I've got to talk it over with my mother," I answered.

"Sounds about right, don't wait too long," he said.

~ * ~

"Sell your horse from under you? What's Sid thinking?" My mom was livid.

"It's an expensive animal, Mom. Worth way more than I knew. I want him sure, but if I can't have him, two thousand is a lot of money. I could help you pay the mortgage."

"Geez Louise, it's a heap of money. But no way is anyone taking that money from you. You worked for it, Shells. You can buy a cheaper horse. We will make it work. I swear, no one's going to take this farm from us. We have the land, the stalls, the water rights, an artesian well, and the know-how. Your Dad was gung-ho about you barrel racing. If you want to do it."

"I want a horse, Mom. My own horse. I'm already in training. I'll have money to pay training fees. I'll get an older horse, so I can start right away. Watch me, I'll help you keep the farm."

"You're just like your Dad," Mom said, staring at me. "It's a deal. Let's shake 'em up, show them what the McMurdle's are made of." She held out her hand. I took it, and grasped it hard, like my Dad had taught me. Hold on hard, then when you're good and ready, let go.

~ * ~

I let Sid know my decision, accepted the two thousand, and asked if I could have a steady paying job, not a trade. He looked at me with his eyes squinched up. Twelve hours a week, after school and holidays, more hours when vacation's on.

He nodded. "Okay. Done. But no spending extra time on that colt, hear."

I shook my head no.

"You can start whenever you want then."

"I want to be paid in cash on Fridays like the other fellas."

"Your eyes aren't closed, are they? Fair enough." And that was that.

~ * ~

In the school library I looked up where I could buy a horse for the money I had and it was slim pickings. More like worn out husks. Old horses in need of homes, horses too big, too broad for barrel racing.

Then I read about the Bureau of Land Management selling horses and burros from their roundups. I've heard about the BLM all my life, about as long as I had been riding. They had fans and mud-slingers on both sides of the fence. You could adopt a mustang and train it. A mustang was a perfect barrel horse size. But the next auction was a long time away and I still needed to train my possible adopted horse. I didn't have years, I had months. And I needed to enter a barrel race as soon as possible. Even so, I signed up to adopt a mustang.

The worse part of working at Sid's farm, was, as you probably guessed, watching the little squirt whose father bought my colt. Sid asked me to give him some pointers, but I'd point blank refused. Wicket kept wondering why I wasn't working him, kept calling me whenever he saw me.

Plum wore me out.

Not being on a ranch, city slickers don't know this, but most kids know how to drive cars, trucks, tractors by the time they are eight. My Dad had taught me how to drive. Sid needed me to know how to drive a tractor and was having Ray teach me the basics, not that it was complicated. Turn the key, shift gears, etc. But a bit of a problem when you are short, like me. Which nobody ever mentions because if anybody had ever mentioned the word, "Shorty," Dad'd given them the what-for stare and said, "I'll shorten you." Kept me safe for about five square miles.

Ray was edging towards tying a brick to my foot to make it longer, then said, "Maybe I'll have a talk with Sid. This is expecting too much. Hey, heard you were looking for a BLM horse, yah?"

"Yah," I said, slipping out of the hard tractor seat to the ground.

"There's an older woman three farms to the west who bought two mustangs, but she can't work them anymore. She bought them both as foals and had good luck with them. You might want to talk to her."

"You mean Leah?" Leah was always up in arms about every wrongdoing done to man or animals and had quite a reputation. Mostly folks stayed clear of her.

"Yes," Ray nodded. "Here's her number."

"Why do you have her number?"

"She might just be able to help you out. Besides, she's a friend of mine, but don't tell anybody," Ray said "Capiche?"

~ * ~

After an awkward phone call, my mom drove me to meet Leah and just what we might be taking on. Beige dust blew out behind us on the dirt road.

A small woman, only as tall as me, was sitting on her front porch drinking something long and cool and clinking in a tall glass on her porch. Mom and I got out. The woman stood up, set her cowboy hat on her head, and stepped off her porch, holding a cane.

"Pleased to meet you." She nodded at me, then at Mom. "And to see you, again, Grace. Sure sorry to hear about Merle."

Mom nodded her head, still unable to say anything when people mentioned Dad.

"Let's go look at some horses," Leah said, thumping her cane on the ground.

Nearing a corral next to her house she whistled. Two horses trotted round the side of the barn. One of them was caramel-colored with black mane and tail, looked like a grown-up Wicket wearing a wig. She had a star on her forehead. The other horse was more dun-colored. Both of them had small sturdy black hooves, shining as though they were just polished. Leah noticed me looking at their hooves. "They hardly need trimming, their hooves are so perfect," she said. "They will work well for you if you treat them right. Moonbeam here," she said pointing to the one that looked like Wicket, "doesn't like fireworks or firecrackers or any loud explosion sounds. Neither of them like horseflies, have quite a strong aversion to them. I make a solution of diluted cider vinegar ten-to-one that works well to spray on. Horseflies make them twitchy. But, if you remember to use the vinegar, they'll behave very well."

"We were just looking, Miss Leah," I said.

"I heard tell you needed a horse for barrel racing. And when I signed the paperwork on adopting my two mustangs, they said I could find them new homes if I needed to, but I would officially need to approve their new home. And the BLM does too. I officially approve you as their new owner if you would like them, and the BLM has heard of your family, because the McMurdles Farm has a fine reputation. So, you're good to go there. And Ray has told me what a fine job you done gentling the colt you call Wicket. I think you are the perfect person. What do you say?"

I looked at her and then my Mom. She pushed her auburn bangs away from her eyes, where tears were brimming. She nodded yes.

"Did you know about this?" I asked.

"I had no idea, but I think it's perfect," Mom said.

"I only have two thousand dollars, Miss Leah. I can work off the rest if they cost more."

"Oh no, Dear," she laughed, leaning on her cane. "These horses have to go together so you'd be doing me a favor. I'd be honoring my deal in adopting them and giving them a good home. They work well separately and away from each other, but I'd be happier knowing they were together. I don't want any money from you. None a'tall. I want to see what they become when you work with them. I've taken a spin around a barrel in my time, and I think you are made for each other."

I hadn't cried at all since Dad died and I hadn't cried when I had to give up Wicket, but I fought back tears now.

"Can I meet them first, please?"

"Be my guest."

I undid the latch on the tall wooden fence and walked in. The one she called Moonbeam walked over to me and pushed on my belly with her nose, looking for a nose rub. The other one nuzzled me on my back as I scratched Moonbeam's nose. I turned around and started walking in a circle around the fence, so I could clamber up it if I needed to, truth be told. I felt the thudding of two pairs of hooves through my boots as I walked, and turned around. Both horses were willingly following me.

"Sold," I said placing my hands on both their noses.

"They come with saddles, reins, blankets, vitamins, even cider vinegar. And one caveat. You'll ride over here sometime to let me know how they are doing. Or invite me to visit them."

"I can do that," I said. I wouldn't be a good horsewoman if I didn't ask to ride them under saddle. To be sure. Before I broke my heart again. Under saddle, both of them were feisty, but well-behaved.

"Would you look at that," Leah said, standing by Mom. "Everything's going to work out well, you'll see."

"Have the second sight do you, Leah?"

"No, Grace, just common sense. Just like you." I couldn't believe it as Leah nudged Mom in the hip like they were doing a reggae dance called The Bump Mom had once showed me that was danced to songs by Bob Marley and the Wailers.

~ * ~

So, I ended up with two horses of my own. I was so busy I didn't have time to work for Sid anymore. Or see Wicket. Mom said I was a motivated worker, so she paid me for keeping correct school hours. I got a second job at Food City on weekend mornings because they had such trouble getting people to work here, out in the middle of nowhere Montana. Then it was summer and barrel racing season started in earnest for me—competitions are all year long, but I'm still in school.

Early one morning, Leah arrived unexpectedly carrying a battered canvas bag, holding a stopwatch in the middle of her hand that hung on a silver chain around her neck. "Time to get to work there, Shelby, set up the barrels. Tell Reno to do it, they are too heavy for you to be lifting. Rather, *ask* Reno to do it, don't forget to say *please*. I'm going in to give salutations to your mother." She headed towards the house, leaning on her cane. Half an hour later, Mom and Leah walked out.

"Shells, meet your new coach." Mom flung out her hand, as if announcing Leah. "Barrel racing champion nineteen seventy-four and seventy-five. Best kept secret round here."

"When you've aggravated people as much as I have, they don't remember the good stuff," Leah said. "Who goes first, Moonbeam or Rocket?"

"Geez Louise, that's Moonbeam's new name. She seems to like it," I answered.

"Works for me. The judges will check the barrels are in the right place. We'll pretend they've already done that. Before next time, you'll need to mark out the distances, so they are set apart same as you'll find them in an arena, duplicating the circuit. You have one minute—sixty seconds—to complete a figure eight around the course, one time around each barrel. Your goal is to do it in fifteen to thirty seconds. You're young yet. You can bump the barrel but if it moves and upends, a five-second penalty will be assessed. If you don't complete the course, it counts as no time. You come shooting into the ring and go shooting out of the ring. Sounds easy, doesn't it?

"Get your gear on, girl. Ready to ride."

Pretty soon, Geez Louise and I stand ready at attention.

"Why do you want to win, Shelby McMurdle?"

"I like to win," I answer, looking at Mom, wondering if I can speak the truth. Mom shrugs.

"But, *why* do you want to win, Shelby McMurdle?" Leah insists.

"To save our farm. Earn enough money to pay the mortgage. Keep it."

"Excellent. Pure survival as motivation. Your mustangs understand this completely. Their wish to win when racing against others is pure survival. You will be racing against no other horses, only against the clock in the ring, but you must convey your wish, funnel your survival instincts through the reins to your horse, so you can work together. I just have to say, I forgot to warn you your mustangs will stamp snakes, javelinas, and other creatures, as a result of having been born in the wild. I adopted them at six months. They had a whole storehouse of knowledge by then. So be aware, a horse shying while under saddle may have a real reason, it may not just be misbehavior.

"Close your eyes, see if you can get any messages or information from your horse. It's part of being a team."

Right away, the message I received, probably because I wondered it myself, and, feeling off the wall as I repeated it, was, "She wonders why you are not standing by her, petting her, and she wonders where the molasses nuggets are that you carry."

"Excellent. That sounds accurate. You are her owner now. I cannot pet her without your permission. The molasses nuggets are in my pocket and she probably smells them. That's enough for a starting point. Now, walk her slowly around the barrels circling each one as you form a figure eight. You know the drill, but she doesn't."

At the end of the lesson, "Permission to pet your horse, and bestow a treat, please," Leah said. She walked over, patted Geez Louise on the nose as she gave her a molasses nugget. "You read her right, Shelby, I truly think so."

~ * ~

Wednesday and Sunday mornings Leah arrived with her stop-watch, checking in with Mom, and then coaching me.

The mind-meld thing sounded as crazy as it did in the old Star Trek reruns but it helped me think more about how Geez Louise understood her world, and how to communicate better with my legs and hands. I wore spurs but found my horse understood me without my using them. She didn't like the quirt either, in fact, when I used the quirt is the only time she bucked. Bucked me right off.

"What did you learn from that?" Leah asked, looking up at the sky as though even looking at the sky was "a teachable moment."

"She doesn't like being smacked."

"Would you?" Leah faced me.

I don't like being bucked off and it wouldn't win me points so, using the quirt was out.

"She also hates the spurs," I added.

"Any reason why?"

"They feel like a horsefly biting? They hurt?"

"Bingo! If you are already armed with the knowledge she hates being bitten by horseflies, why annoy her by imitating a really big horsefly?"

"It will look wimpy if I don't wear them."

"Carry on," Leah said, letting it drop for now.

I have to admit, it's easy to get discouraged training just with a coach and Mom watching under a big vast sky. The first meet is coming up though. One more month. Past our bank deadline, but Mom had talked them into a three-month extension. Mom said she was too busy to bake anything for a fundraising cake sale when neighbors told her they were holding one for us. After the cake sale, they proudly handed over three hundred dollars.

At the end of the lesson, Leah said, "When I rode, I taught myself. I used the quirt, spurs, anything to win. We were all rough. I didn't think about how my horse thought, not till later. I wonder what it would have been like to give myself permission to connect with my horse more than I did. Sure, everyone's different and rides

different, but you have that permission now. Use all your understanding. Then give it all you got, and win."

~ * ~

Wednesday, Mom came out as Leah arrived, opened her trunk
and started carrying out a battery-operated boombox, and an
umbrella. Mom pulled out a folding chair and set it up for Leah.
"Thanks." Leah nodded, propping up her umbrella over her head,
inserting the handle on a holder on the chair. It was six A.M., but
already the sun was strong.

"Today we are adding noise that you'd find on the circuit. Out
here it's quiet, which I like, the horses like, but they have to get
accustomed to music and noise. They've heard tractors, crop dusters,
backfires, but we need more. Every time you do a circuit, turn this
thing on, when you do your chores, turn this on."

Mercy Holler the DJ for KPFM came through loud and clear,
then a song from Big and Rich. Geez Louise tossed her head. "She
might know this song, I played the radio loud enough at my house,"
Leah said with a laugh. "After three circuits with her, I want you out
here riding Rocket, and Geez Louise waiting her turn, get her used to
waiting and standing still while saddled up."

Rocket seemed to like the radio, and danced a little sideways,
performing a perfect figure eight the first time.

"He's going with you when you compete, as your back up
horse," Leah said.

I looked over at Mom. She nodded. "Plenty of room."

"They will also keep each other calm, be a cushion," Leah said.

The radio played all week long, and made chores seem shorter.
Sunday rolled around and people started driving up, before Leah.
Ray and his son Gary got out of his truck, Erma from Food City
and a couple other people. Leah got out of her Dodge Rambler.
"This here's your cheering section. Free admission. Consider it your
first performance, *unofficially*."

Our hired hands, Ryan and Luis, appeared too.

Ray and Gary took the card table Mom was carrying out, set it
up, went back in, came out carrying a jug of sweet tea, paper cups,
and boxes of donuts. Looking over at me, it was the first time I had
seen her smile since Dad died.

She walked over, still smiling. "I was going to give this to you to wear the morning of your first event, but since this is your first event, *unofficially*, lend me your neck for a minute."

I leaned down from the saddle and she reached up, fastening the clasp of Dad's Saint Sebastian medal around my neck, the one he always wore. "It brought him luck. You bring us luck. It's yours now."

Leah, set up on her chair complete with umbrella, turned on the radio. The men hollered and Erma clapped her hands. Mom held her hands against her face as if in surprise. "Next up, Shelby McMurdle. Go," Leah said, clicking the stopwatch.

Geez Louise jumped forward. Greased lightning as she curled me round the three barrels, leaning so far into the corners I thought we'd slide onto the ground, then out the faux entrance posts. "Perfect time, she wins!" Leah called.

Ray and Gary threw up their hats, Erma yodeled, and Mom said as if on cue, "Geez Louise!"

~ * ~

I'd been growing so fast we ordered a new pair of Wranglers, western dress shirt, and a pair of size five-and-a-half boots for me. My hat would do fine. They arrived in the mail just two days before my event, fit perfectly. I was still short though, 5 foot 1 instead of 4 foot 11. Perfect size for a barrel rider. With a perfect caramel-colored horse, short just like I am. Shortish.

It's June 29. Williston, North Dakota's rodeo is a two-hour drive away from our Montana ranch. Most people make it a long weekend but for us, it will be a day trip. Ryan hitched the trailer to the truck as Mom stuffed our suitcases into the back seat. A supply of water, hay, molasses nuggets and the vinegar horsefly spray were packed in the trailer's side hatch.

Check list: saddle, saddle pad, reins, saddle soap, curry comb, brush, bucket, extra spray bottle. Check.

Check list: jeans, boots, hair scrunchie, hairbrush, shampoo, aspirin, registration papers. Check.

We were getting in the truck cab when Leah drove up, opened her trunk. "I'll get that," Mom said, carrying out her suitcase, chair, and umbrella.

"You didn't think you'd compete without me there, did ya?"

She and Mom faced me, smiling.

"Let's go, girls." Leah grabbed the sidebar, hauled herself up, stopwatch swinging forward on its chain below her collarbone.

~ * ~

So here I am. Geez Louise's muscles tremble as I hold her still in the alley. My back number reads 5 and is firmly attached to my new western shirt. I wanted number 7, but you can't have everything. Geez Louise is not the horse I was promised. She is the horse I was given: a surprise. We're waiting in the alley, reins firmly held in my two hands.

We're next in line, then they call number 5. Geez Louise shoots into the ring like a rocket, my other horse's name. We lean towards the first barrel, circle it, her hoofbeats ringing in my ears as I count them, count out the strides to the next barrel, circle it, head toward the last barrel. The crowd is yelling, loudspeakers blaring canned music, Geez Louise stretches towards the barrel, beginning to circle it. Then there's blasts of firecrackers, and she stumbles, her foreleg catching. Someone's celebrating the 4th of July early. She rights herself but I continue her stumble, my head falling onto the 55-gallon metal barrel. *This is not supposed to happen*, I think as my head and shoulder crash the barrel, knock it over, then Geez Louise stretches out her left foreleg, rights us both, as I straighten my back, maintaining the curve and we're out the ring. Knocking the barrel over is a 5-second penalty but doesn't count as a no time. We still count.

Someone hands my hat to me. We walk down the alley, away from those waiting for their run, to await the results. My head is pounding and something's wrong with my shoulder, but we still count. I try to punch my hat to reshape it, but my left arm doesn't want to move.

The medic comes to check me out, regulations. Get off? Now? Someone holds the reins as I pull my feet out of the stirrups, bring my right foot around, and slide off. Not a good idea. I know what's wrong, seen it before, with my Dad. Broken collarbone. Medic shines the light in my eyes, concussion, confirms I need an X-ray, probably a Cat-scan. Then Mom and Leah are there, they aren't supposed to be, but they've talked their way in. Mom holds Geez Louise and Leah walks next to me, out of the alley to the rodeo doctor's office. He has to sign me off as medically unable to compete in the next round and finalize transport for me to the hospital. Then my name is called: "Number 5, Shelby McMurdle on Geez Louise, places third."

I placed third! It's not first though, not what I wanted.

I rode to win. To save the farm.

Leah looks at me. "But what did you learn?" she asks.

"Geez Louise righted us both, she had my back."

"Yes." Leah raised her tightly held right fist in a stance of triumph. "That she did. She's got your back. Some horses, like people, don't give a fig for anyone else, but she does. Bravo."

Third prize is only $250, doesn't cover fees or gas money.

"We've already discussed it. Leah will ride with you to the hospital, and I'll arrange for someone to stay with the horses until we get back, meet you there. Then back here, trailer up, home we go. Third place is great, Shells. Just wish you weren't hurt." Mom bit her lip.

~ * ~

Collar bones heal fast. But you can't ride until they do, doctors say. Doctors don't know the McMurdles, do they. So, I don't ride but I keep all the moves in my mind, lead Geez Louise and Rocket, keep my hand in, talk to them.

I miss the next meet but am ready for my next practice and finally call Leah to let her know. Someone whose voice I don't recognize answers. "I'll see if she can come to the phone," she says.

"Shells, how's tricks?" Leah sounds tired.

"Who's the person there?"

"Nosy as always, huh," Leah says. "Let me speak to your mother."

"Mom," I call, "it's Leah."

Mom grasps the phone, listens. "Okay. We'll be right over," she says then hangs up. "Time to take a ride, Shells."

"Right now?"

"Leah wants to talk to you. She'll explain."

~ * ~

We drive up the dusty road. Leah is sitting on the front porch like before, but she doesn't get up. She is sitting in a wheelchair. The sound of our doors closing echo like slams as we approach her.

There's only one other chair. "Sit down. Long time no see," Leah said.

Impatient, I said nothing, waiting. "You're reading me right, Dear. Stage four lung cancer; just had a breathing treatment so I can talk. Don't worry. I'll stop when I'm ready. A few more weeks, that's it. Coaching you was the best thing that's happened to me in a long time." She coughed and the nurse wheeled out an oxygen tank and mask.

"Told you to sit inside," the nurse admonished her.

Leah waved her free hand as the other held her oxygen mask to her face. She allowed the nurse to fit a plastic tube into her nose. "Breathe in," the nurse said. "I told her this was too much, but she wants to talk to you out here."

I hadn't noticed how gray Leah's face was until a little color seeped into it. She waved her hand, and the nurse took the mask away from her face but she stood there at the ready. "Pretend I'm not here," she said as Leah rolled her eyes.

"Cliff notes, then. Geez Louise, Rocket, in best place God could ever imagine. Been thinking about him lately, God. Best girl ever to train them. God's gift. That's you Shells." She coughed and the nurse gave her more oxygen, mist spraying her mouth and nose.

I looked at Mom. "Did you know?"

"Reading you now, and no, she didn't know. No one but Ray. Easier that way. We had fun, didn't we? You rode so well. Third place. I'm so proud." She coughed, and more oxygen was given.

"That's enough. I'm sorry," the nurse said.

Leah raised her hand and took the oxygen mask away from her mouth. "Thank you for taking my horses, I can go knowing they are well taken care of. You have been a blessing. Come see me again." She coughed again.

Mom leaned over and gave her a tiny hug.

I was afraid I'd hurt her. "I won't break," Leah said, reaching out both her hands. She set her stopwatch on the silver chain in mine. She closed her hands together over mine with a touch as gentle as moth wings, in a prayerful position, then squeezed tightly, just once, and let go.

I watched as the nurse pushed her away through the front door.

"Come back tomorrow," the nurse said.

But the next day, Leah was unconscious when Mom called to arrange another visit. Mom asked if it was alright if we sat with her and the nurse agreed.

On our way over, Leah met the angels.

~ * ~

The nurse was wiping away tears as she opened the door. "She'd be happy that you were here," she said.

Leah looked so tiny, lying there, her gray hair brushed, long on the pillow. The oxygen tubing was coiled up like a lariat on the side of the oxygen tank, her face was freshly washed, and the smell of roses was in the air from two bouquets on her side table.

"That's what she wanted," the nurse said, "Roses. They're from Ray. I've just called him. That's it. No one else. You two and him. Take your time. I set out two chairs. I'll be in the other room."

Mom looked at her, at the chairs, and me, shook her head, no. "Me either," I said. "But could you open the window for her? She loved the outdoors."

The nurse nodded. "Long as there's screens." A slight breeze blew in as we left.

We drove back in silence. I couldn't help thinking, Leah's gone and we're going to lose the farm. I tried so hard. I couldn't see a way around it.

I saddled up Geez Louise and led Rocket on the mile-long walk down to our mailbox. "This walk is for you, Leah," I said.

Then I got on with my chores.

~ * ~

There weren't many people at Leah's funeral. Her people were gone. Ray was there, Erma, Ryan and Luis, Mom, all the people from my *unofficial* competition, and a man we didn't recognize dressed in a dark gray suit.

After Leah was buried, the man in the dark gray suit approached me and Mom. "Hello, Mrs. McMurdle, Shelby. I'm Roy Bannister, Leah Lister's lawyer. Do you have a minute?"

Mom glanced at me. "We have chores to do, Mr. Bannister, if it's all the same to you, we must get home."

"Then here." He tried to hand us a thick beige envelope. "I'll be brief. Leah Lister had no family. You may know she lived on her family's land going back three generations, lost her husband, a veteran?"

"Mr. Bannister, this is not the time."

"She said to say, *I'm reading you.* And to be quick. She's left everything to Shelby in a trust. Just so you know she was of sound mind. She called me the first day you visited her farm together to set everything up. I can explain more later. She wants you to not lose *your* farm, Mrs. McMurdle. She has to have a place to keep Geez Louise and Rocket. Did I not say their names right?" he asked as Mom started laughing.

"We've given you more than a minute, wouldn't you say, Mr. Bannister?" Mom reached out her hand, touched my arm. "We're going to be all right, Shells."

"I'm reading you, now, Leah Lister," Mom said softly before smiling at Mr. Bannister. "We'll let Leah have the last say. I think she'd like that. Mr. Bannister, we are on our way to a tiny gathering at our house for Leah right now. Please join us and tell us all about it afterward, if that's what she wanted."

~ * ~ * ~

Sara Brett has published widely with an international audience.

HABLA ESPAÑOL?
IF YOU RODEO—YOU DO!

Richard L. Carrico

What could be more a slice of Americana than a good old rodeo? The clothing, the hats, the hardware, special ropes, the swagger of the cowgirls and cowboys, and even the rodeo language itself sets it apart from any other sport. The word *rodeo* itself is a Spanish word meaning a circular place where cattle are exhibited or branded. Be *savvy* (from Spanish *sabe*, to know) to our rodeos' rich and colorful language, a lot of it derived from Spanish and Mexican words.

We all know cowpokes, cattle, and rodeos are a uniquely western United States phenomena. The roots of dusty cattle drives, and competitive roping extend deep into our history. So deep, that in some cases, time has erased the richness of rodeo vernacular. Let's brush off some of that historical dust.

Feel like imitating Clint Eastwood from one of his spaghetti westerns? Slip your *poncho* over your head and top it off with your favorite well-worn wide-brimmed *sombrero*. And speaking of hats, that ten-gallon Stetson of yours does not take its name from the American gallon, but instead from a Spanish *galón* which is a braided or twinned decoration like a hat band. Need to wipe some sweat from your forehead or shine up your conchos? Use your *bandana*, a Spanish word for scarf.

Maybe for protection of your legs you wear a weathered set of *chaps*, a Spanish word borrowed from either *chaparreras* or *chaparajos*. Just remember—the ch is pronounced closer to an s not hard like the ch in chapter. On your stirrups you might have *tapaderos*, more commonly called taps, which are leather coverings to shield your feet. Maybe you are fashion forward and dress up your chaps or taps by embellishing them with silver or metal *conchas*. *Conchas* or *conchos* derive their name from the Spanish word for seashells or shell-shaped objects.

Out in the *corral*, Spanish for an enclosure, you can fit your *bronco* (Spanish for rough or unpolished) with a *jaquima*, an Arabic word adopted by Spaniards, which you know as a hackamore. You need to cinch (*cincha*, meaning to tighten or tie down) your saddle and try your best to win that coveted shiny championship belt buckle. That bronco, the one you ride, not the one you drive, might be a *pinto*, Spanish for a two-colored horse. Or a *palomino*, from *paloma*, a golden colored dove. That braided quirt in your gloved hand takes its name from *cuarta*, Spanish for horse whip. The ropes you use to control your cattle include *lariats* and *reatas*, both derived from Spanish. A common word that can be both a verb and a noun is lasso from the Spanish *lazo*. That loop or eye at the end of your lasso is often called a *honda* or *hondo*, make sure it is secure.

Away from the rodeo or corral and out on the range you might come across a herd of galloping mustangs, from Spanish *mesteño* meaning wild or not claimed. The herd of mustangs might be led by a seemingly clever or intelligent *ladino*, a learned one. We are talking horses here, not automobiles. Hopefully while out on the open range, your cattle herd doesn't *estampida*, you know, stampede.

Maybe you are young and just starting out on the rodeo circuit or on a ranch (derived from *rancho*), that might make you a wrangler from the Spanish word *caballerango*. There is also an old uncommon English word "wrangler" from the sixteenth century but most likely our western American wrangler comes from fifteenth century Spanish. Who knew your favorite pair of jeans has such a heritage. Many a "cowboy" shies away from that term and in some regions, buckaroo (Spanish from *vaquero*) is used instead.

So, put on your *poncho* and maybe your Wrangler jeans and hit the trail *pronto*. I'll see you at the rodeo. I might just be in the stands wearing my favorite old tennis shoes, you know, the pair with the Spanish word for a cougar embossed on the side—*Puma*.

~ * ~ * ~

Richard L. Carrico is an award-winning author, archaeologist, Army veteran, and educator, who grew up in Southern California and has always felt close ties to the land and its people—past and present, on both sides of the Mexican border.

He is the author of four non-fiction books. His award-winning true crime non-fiction book, *Monsters on the Loose* was released by WildBlue Press in late 2023. He has also published *History of Wines and Wineries of San Diego County* (2023); *Images of America Series: Ramona* (2011); *Strangers in a Stolen Land: The Indians of San Diego County from Prehistory to the New Deal* (2014 and 2018) which was the runner-up in the San Diego Book Sellers Best Non-Fiction Category; and *San Diego's Ghosts and Hauntings*. He is currently at work on a book about Spade Cooley, America's Country Western Swing murderer.

Richard has also authored more than 30 publications in professional/academic journals including *American Antiquity*, the *Boletín*, *Journal of San Diego History*, *Pacific Coast Archaeological Society Quarterly*, *Western States Jewish Quarterly*, the *Journal of California and Great Basin Anthropology*, and *Rock Art Papers: Proceedings of the San Diego Rock Art Association*.

In the popular realm of magazine and periodical writing Richard has authored historically or archaeologically based articles for the *San Diego Reader* (March 2023), *San Diego Union*, *Ramona Sentinel*, *California Magazine*, *Ranch and Coast Magazine*, *San Diego Home & Garden*, *SkyWest Inflight Magazine*, *Baja California Magazine*, and others.

RODEO CLOWN VS
HEAVY METAL BAND

John A. Tures

Rodeo clowns play an important role. Their job is to save a rider who is thrown from an angry bull, by getting its attention. It is an act that requires a lot of courage. One time, a short, bandy-legged rodeo clown got the attention of our border town, upset over a racially tinged insult from a heavy metal band that could have torn our city apart. He refocused our anger using humor in a way that helped defuse the situation and allowed those rockers who made a terrible mistake to apologize. It also paved the way for our city's unity in the wake of its worst tragedy decades later.

~ * ~

In this story, I'm not a cowboy or clown. I'm just a kid who loves rodeo and hard rock, and I'll never forget the day my favorite rodeo clown bested my favorite metal band. It was the funniest thing you ever saw. It wasn't until I was an adult that I realized how important that moment was, after a terrible tragedy hit our town in 2019.

Growing up a military brat I came from Wisconsin to Texas because of my dad's deployment to the border. But it didn't take long to learn from my newfound friends what a rodeo was, or how big a deal it could be.

Within the first year of living in El Paso, my parents took me, my brothers and sister and my neighborhood pal Rene Gonzalez to my first Southwest International Livestock Show and Rodeo. I knew about most of these animals because my dad was raised on a dairy farm, but I had never seen riding or rope tricks. It turns out these events had been going on in the U.S. since the 1800s. In Spanish class, we learned "rodeo" meant "to go around" or "encircle." A history teacher showed us pictures of Mexican Vaqueros doing rope tricks and horsemanship games. We later learned Western cowboys engaged in similar fun after great cattle drives. Think of the term "round-up."

Nearly everyone in El Paso got in on the act. We learned about the care of these animals in 4H, where I once witnessed a horse's surgery. The week of the rodeo, we went to the town square to see the parade the Sheriff's Department and Chamber of Commerce put on.

El Paso has quite the history of being a tough Wild West Town. It's a history that includes John Wesley Hardin, the most notorious killer of the Old West. Hardin has been credited with perhaps the most murders of any gunman, and even bragged about killing a man for snoring. He was eventually gunned down in a saloon in our border town a year before our town's first rodeo. El Paso is also not far from Lincoln County and Billy the Kid fame. Sheriff Pat Garrett, Billy the Kid's killer, was gunned down near Las Cruces, New Mexico, the next town over. And there's the Marty Robbins classic country ballad that begins with "Out in the West Texas town of El Paso…"

Every year at the rodeo we saw cowboys enter the bareback and saddle bronc riding, calf-roping, steer wrestling, and the cowgirls with the barrel racing event. In Boy Scouts, I put what I had learned watching those ladies into action and took third place in a New Mexico rodeo event in a version of barrel racing where you had to grab three flags from the top of the three large barrels, and not knock them down. Truth be told, I did so well because I had a horse that was smart.

They even had events for kids, like a "pig wrestling contest," where a family friend made it to the finals of the contest before the hog simply shook off the tiny wrangler and casually sauntered out of the ring, to laughter from the onlookers.

Halfway through the rodeo, we'd see a Country-Western concert with an old legend or a young buck, featured on KHEY, the local C&W station. They turned out the lights and we'd twirl our glow sticks, a great effect when thousands of attendees do it at once. It was like Super Bowl week, but for rodeo fans.

But nothing could top the most epic of all rodeo events for kids and adults alike: bull riding.

Unlike our parents, we didn't know many of the names of the cowboys. We knew they had to hang on for dear life for eight seconds, and once the beast hurled them to the ground, the real fun began.

It was time for the rodeo clowns.

And there was one clown in particular who everyone in the city of El Paso absolutely adored: Quail Dobbs.

If you've ever seen the Howard Hawks cinematic masterpiece *Rio Bravo*, starring John Wayne, Angie Dickinson, Dean Martin, and Ricky Nelson, then Quail Dobbs would be a perfect twin of "Stumpy," the aged deputy with the funny high-pitched squeal of a Texas accent played to great laughs by Walter Brennan. It remains my favorite Western no matter what *Yellowstone* film or version of *Lonesome Dove* they come up with these days.

Dobbs had been doing his act for more than two decades. While the other clowns were more agile, running, waving flags, dodging, and jumping up into the stands to get away from the angry bull, Dobbs was a barrelman. He'd move those stubby little legs around, get the bull to chase him, and dive into the safety of the barrel in the nick of time. Kids would howl with laughter when Dobbs popped his legs out of the bottom of the barrel. Then he would creep around the bull like a tank.

As great as that act was, the best part was when he brought in two additional "clowns." One was a mannequin that was lowered from the ceiling by a rope. A bull could knock that dummy dozens of feet in the air while the cowboy climbed his way to safety. But the other clown was the one we looked forward to every year.

Before the bull and rider gate would open, Quail Dobbs would engage in some banter with the announcer, just like Stumpy arguing with John Wayne's sheriff in *Rio Bravo*. Dobbs would drag out a scarecrow dressed as a rodeo clown. Since there was no pole to hold the scarecrow upright, Dobbs also brought out a broom, jabbing the figure upright in a most embarrassing spot, which would make the audience roar with laughter.

In their back-and-forth, the announcer would ask the name of the scarecrow clown. And Dobbs supplied the name of a less-than-popular politician.

In the late 1970s, with rampant inflation, President Jimmy Carter took a turn at having his name attached to the scarecrow. After him, the scarecrow-clown was given the name "Bill Clements" after our gaffe-prone GOP governor. During an early 1980s economic recession, with his approval ratings in the mid-30s, Ronald Reagan became the luckless scarecrow clown. Then Democratic Texas Governor Mark White, the man who beat Clements, got an unfortunate chance to be a clown for a night, probably because he raised taxes. Texans hate those. Young and old got to laugh loudly at both the use of the broom, and the way a bull would knock the stuffing out of the scarecrow clown.

With two Democrats and two Republicans as guest clowns and the embarrassing broom propping them up, you had to admit: Dobbs was pretty bipartisan in his political mocking.

But one night, he changed everything with a different name for his special clown.

~ * ~

When our metal music switched from record albums to cassette tapes, the first one I bought was Def Leppard's "Pyromania." This British metal band had hits I loved, from "Photograph" to "Rock of Ages" to "Foolin.'" And a friend helped me dub their album "High and Dry" onto a blank cassette. I remember calling MTV to vote for "Photograph" in the Friday Night Video fight. The band even came to El Paso for a raucous concert, promoted by my favorite rock station, KLAQ on September 6, 1983.

Then everything changed.

We learned that after leaving our Texas border town, Def Leppard went on to Tucson, Arizona. For some reason, the fans out there just didn't get into the music like those in our city did. Singer Joe Elliot wasn't pleased. According to media reports Elliot allegedly said, "Last night, we played in El Paso, that place with all of the greasy Mexicans, and they made a lot more noise than that." Another guy in the band reportedly cringed at the words.

Just so you know, just about everyone at my school, my soccer team, and my Boy Scout Troop, was Hispanic. The overwhelming majority of the town is Hispanic. And yes, everyone in El Paso learned pretty quickly what was said.

Hispanic leaders in El Paso called for a boycott of the band, which our white mayor enthusiastically backed. KLAQ's radio program director publicly ripped up their album cover. I hid my Pyromania cassette and my dub tape as well, embarrassed by that comment. Later, the singer said he was a fan of Cheech and Chong and thought it would be funny.

It wasn't.

The band did apologize, but locals thought it was kind of half-hearted. The whole thing could have gotten ugly. A lot of people had short fuses.

To the outsider, El Paso seems pretty peaceful, but under the surface back then, it was a different story. You'd hear about fights between Hispanic and "Anglo" kids at local schools, as well as teachers taking sides, based on which group they were from. A female friend, who was a neighbor, was beaten up during that time. A teacher told us about the U.S.-Mexican War, and how the gringo and greaser insults began in cross-border battles. The place was like a powder keg, ready to blow.

And then Quail Dobbs stepped in.

~ * ~

At the next rodeo, the Albany, Texas rodeo clown dragged out the scarecrow, as well as his trusty broom to painfully prop up his assistant. When the announcer asked who the assistant clown would be, Dobbs had his answer.

In his heavy Texas accent Dobbs announced, "This here's Def Leppard!"

After a second of shock, the crowd went wild, cheering like crazy. With one line in his show, he got us all laughing our heads off. We roared with delight every time the bull blasted the scarecrow off his feet and after each new jab of the broom.

The next day, at school, everyone who went that night made sure word got out. We must have retold that story a dozen times on the playground. No doubt the adults shared it around water coolers, on buses, and in board meetings.

~ * ~

Def Leppard also changed their tune as well. Unlike a lot of people who say insensitive things, this British heavy metal band got it right. They not only apologized, but I heard Elliot donated money out of his own pocket to a series of Hispanic youth causes. Leaders in El Paso began to tone down the boycott rhetoric. I could soon play Def Leppard songs again. And when their next album, "Hysteria," was released, many of my friends went out and bought it.

Eventually, Def Leppard returned to El Paso to play, and though I had gone off to college by then, I heard it was a great concert. I suppose the hysteria over their comments from 1983 had died down.

I still listen to their greatest hits album these days and took my wife to see them in concert in Truist Park in Atlanta several years ago and cite them as an example of a good, genuine apology.

~ * ~

Normally you wouldn't think this kind of moment mattered, until August 3, 2019. On the darkest day of our city's history, a gunman entered the Wal-Mart in Cielo Vista Mall and opened fire with an AK-47. When the dust settled, 23 people were murdered, and another 22 were badly wounded. Among those slain were a 15-year-old boy and an 86-year-old woman.

That attack occurred during a celebration for my parents' 50th Wedding Anniversary. But all thoughts of a party quickly vanished. Since we knew so many people in El Paso, we spent much of the day making sure everyone we knew was okay.

It wasn't a local who murdered and injured all those people. The killer, Patrick Crusius, had driven from Allen, Texas. That's a suburb of Dallas, Texas. It's nowhere near El Paso. El Paso is about the same distance from the California border as it is to Dallas. It takes about the same time to drive to St. Louis from Dallas that it takes for someone in Dallas to drive to El Paso.

Before committing this crime, the 21-year-old Crusius had posted some anti-Hispanic rants on a White Supremacist site, the whole "Great Replacement Theory" propaganda that claims Hispanics are "replacing" whites in America, with terms borrowed heavily from Nazi ideology. He told arresting authorities he wanted to kill as many immigrants and Mexicans as possible. Pleading guilty enabled him to evade the death penalty, but he'll face 90 life sentences for the murders and hate crimes.

My brother married his longtime girlfriend, who is Hispanic. Their union is the very thing Crusius decried in his online ethnic purity rant, which seems to have triggered him more than anything to motivate his attack. I bet he hates that they had a kid.

Those who promote hate crimes not only hope to kill and intimidate victims, but also to spur on copycat attacks. In other words, they hope there will be retaliation and escalation.

But El Paso did not turn into a war zone. You didn't see retribution by Hispanics against whites, as Crusius may have hoped for. A big reason for that restraint came because whites and Hispanics had come together when the latter faced insulting speech. You don't build trust and goodwill overnight. It needs to take place over a lengthy time frame. It wasn't just because of the actions of just one white Texan standing up for Hispanic Texans. But it was a key piece.

~ * ~

Dobbs, the man who once wanted to be a cowboy, became one of the most famous rodeo clowns in history. Already having been named the Professional Rodeo Cowboys Association (PRCA) "Clown of the Year" in 1978, he repeated as a winner of that PRCA award in 1988. Teasing the heavy metal band Def Leppard did not hurt his career, as Dobbs was named the "Coors Man in the Can" the following year, and again in 1986. He would go on to earn that moniker twice more, in 1990 and 1993.

Five years later, Dobbs would finally retire. His career spanned more than 35 years, beginning in Minnesota, and stretching from Texas to Wyoming. He would trade his barrel and clown costume for a lawman's job, when he was named Justice of the Peace for Coahoma, Texas. True to form, the PRCA reports Dobbs quipped it wasn't hard to make that transition, since some folks see such political figures as clowns anyway.

The world lost Dobbs in 2014, when he passed away at the age of 72 in Texas. But this rodeo clown is not forgotten, having earned the Donita Barnes Lifetime Achievement Award the year he died.

~ * ~

As I write this manuscript, there is so much division in this country, with no shortage of hate speech. Everything seems to be turning into Us vs Them. I hope people will remember a time when the people of a Texas border town stood together in solidarity when a racially tinged insult could have divided us. I hope they remember how a town came together after a horrific crime was committed by man blinded by his own anger and hatred and refused to let that crime lead us down the path he had followed. And I hope they remember a rodeo clown named Quail Dobbs who was a master of his art and knew how to use humor and comedy to remind us we are more alike than not and helped to bring us all together.

~ * ~ * ~

Growing up in El Paso, Texas **John A. Tures** became a regular newspaper columnist and magazine writer for several news magazines and newspapers across the USA (muckrack.com/john-tures) and scholarly journals. He published "Deep Plots" in *Ariel Chart, International Literary Journal* about a different kind of green cemetery and "Prime Time Crime Drama" in *DeKalb Voices Review* about how a fan of crime dramas has one last murder mystery to solve in her old age: her own. He has a flash fiction "The Sophist" in *Instant Noodles* about what happens when a pair of professors have to grade a well-connected student paper's quest for world domination. His nonfiction piece "Bridge Builders" in Preservation Foundation Inc. tells the story of two African American politicians born centuries apart who found ways to connect people in a variety of ways in the same West Georgia region. Additionally, his story His story "LaGuerrera" was just published by the *Anti-Misogyny Club*. It's about a catcaller who becomes haunted by his victim. Later this year, he'll have "The Propagandist" come out in *YellowMama Press* about a Russian bot farm disunity expert who catches the attention of his superiors. He also has "The Deregulator" coming out in *Down in the Dirt Magazine*, where a red tape cutter experiences the consequences of his policies.

His Twitter or "X" handle is @johnntures2.

THE RELEASE

CL Prater

"Always a good time, Ricky!

"Love your stories!"

"Come down to the Cove for a cold one, It's on Trevor!"

Ricky tipped his hat to the rambunctious group of cowboys and cowgirls. "Don't you close that place down...get some sleep." His growl ended in a chuckle. He was too old, maybe too wise to stay out as late as this younger generation. He noted their clothes as he watched them jostle and tease each other through the back gate. You had to rodeo in brand names now, he guessed. No going to the local farm store to buy feed, a shirt, and jeans in one trip. It was still the way he shopped.

Kay, his cousin, had shook her head at him last Christmas. "Eeh ...you wear the clothes of an old man...put this on." She threw him a sparkly bag tied with ribbon. Untying it, he pulled out a flowered western shirt.

"Think I'm going to Hawaii?" He laughed, holding it up.

Mona, his mother giggled behind her hand. Ricky had actually worn it a couple of times, even got some compliments. He still preferred plain white or a chambray blue for rodeos. He didn't like words down the sleeve either, just plain.

What hadn't changed was the way these young bucks and does loved listening to stories of the old days. He'd gathered plenty of those. They loved to hear about the old-time stars, especially the ones who'd gotten their start right here in this arena. He was proud to acknowledge he'd roped, ridden, and even trained with some of them.

The distant bawl of calves down for the night made him smile. It was his thirty-first year managing this place. He closed the back gate and walked across the soft, freshly harrowed dirt, heading for the electric box to shut off the lights. He heard a snap. The arena went black.

"Alright you clowns," he called, "...turn 'em back on...this old man's got to see."

Silence. Even the calves were still.

His eyes slowly adjusted to the faint moonlight. "If I don't get my work done tonight, none of you'll be riding tomorrow." He knew his threat was weak. His eyes and ears strained for movement, sound. Nothing.

The moon's faint light drew his eyes to the row of chutes. Ricky focused on number one. He always turned to number one.

A sudden scrape of hinges pierced the air. His brain barely made sense of it before the raspy spring of a chute gate followed. Instinct launched him into motion.

Leaping, scrambling, his boots caught the rungs of the nearest panel. The bucking of a bronc, front hooves pummeling the ground, the heaving snort as back legs kicked out, and forelegs returned to push against earth, repeated again and again in thumping beats. He threw his legs over the top rung, falling into a protective crouch. His heart pulsed in his ears. The story he never told, flooded his brain.

He'd pushed it so far back he'd thought it was gone. The bronc's snarling thunder echoed in his ears as he remembered how they both went down. The two of them tumbled, tangled, their heads so close Ricky saw the rolling eyes, felt the spray of snort.

There was another snap and Ricky forced his eyes open; the lights were back on. He stared at the chutes. All of them were closed. Silent, empty, the dark canopy of sky covered the arena like a circus tent. His hands shook as he pulled himself up, glancing embarrassedly around for witnesses. There was no one in the arena. He saw the deep hoof prints dotting the dirt exactly where he'd heard them.

Gelatin legs got him to his pickup. Out of breath, Ricky pulled his phone out of the console, breathed in and punched numbers with a trembling crooked forefinger. "Mom?" Ricky's voice was thick with emotion.

"You saw him, again, didn't you?" Despite her age, Mona had a clear, steady voice.

"Heard him." He whispered hoarsely.

"And you know he'll keep coming back." She paused, giving Ricky time to think. When he didn't respond, she continued. "These aren't flashbacks, son...you know this. You've got to release him."

"But it's Round-Up week...I've got..."

"No...don't wait Ricky...you don't know what could happen."

Ricky let out a slow sigh. "I'll just...I'll let you know, Mom.

Thanks." He punched the red button and closed his eyes. He swallowed dust and started coughing. He still wanted, still needed the comfort of his mother, but something inside him would not cave to her old beliefs.

He got out and unlatched his pickup's tailgate. Sliding his cooler to him, he popped it open and pulled out a bottle of cold water. He chugged until his brain started to freeze. Even a headache was better.

Head throbbing, he willed his legs to keep moving. He needed to shut off the arena lights. Passing by the hollows and hoof prints he tried not to look. How could spirit take on flesh? With shaking hands, he unlocked the box and threw the switch. He took the long way through pens to get back to his pickup; the gravel lanes were better lit.

The next day was a blur of activity. He set up, directed, buzzed his four-wheeler back and forth from pens to arena to concessions to the front gate. A service truck pulled up alongside him. Pete, the electrician, stuck his head out the window.

"Hey Ricky? I got the call to check out the arena lights...from what I can see they're fine. I even checked the lines running to concessions. Freezers and coolers are all working."

"Thanks, Pete." Ricky nodded, his smile hiding disappointment. He wanted to stay rooted in the here and now. He wanted what happened last night to have an explanation.

"You bet Ricky...have a good show."

Parking his four-wheeler behind the concession stand, Ricky breathed in the smell of fresh popcorn. He stuck his head in the snack shack.

"You better grab one now...I can't keep up!" Lynne said pouring a tin cup of kernels tinkling into the popper. Her cheeks were red with heat.

"That's a good thing." Ricky grinned, pulling a brimming bag from the nearly empty crate. "Thanks, ladies, and gents...you're the best!" he called out to his crew.

He fell into step behind the line of mutton-busting tykes, the breeze flapping the numbers on their backs like capes. They rounded concessions, entering the arena through the main gate. Seeing the tiny cowpokes, the bleachers erupted in chuckles and coos.

Ricky grinned as he leaned against a post, munching popcorn, watching Rex, the clown. His oversized wranglers held up by suspenders, revealed his standard polka-dot underwear. Rex lunged, stealing the first little rider's hat as the sheep loped past. The sheep bolted and the little guy fell. Riha, one of the bullfighters, helped the cowboy up, dusted him off, then threw a loop and snagged Rex. He and the tyke pulled Rex back.

"I think that little cowboy deserves a re-ride," Larry, the announcer said with a chuckle. The pit in Ricky's stomach was forgotten.

The next five went down fast. A ribbon and a concession stand certificate, generally dried tears and brought a smile to streaked little faces. The sixth, a little guy as wide as he was tall, made it almost to the end of the arena before the pickup guys intervened. The crowd roared as they peeled him off the sheep like Velcro.

The next little waiting cowgirl had a pink ribbon as big as her head. She was crying, clinging to her grandma's leg. The grandma was pulling her close when Ricky heard the guttural snort. A shock wave split through his veins.

Hooves crashed against planks and the twisting head of a bronc arched wildly over the stock gate. The gateman was not at his post. With the speed of a much younger cowboy, Ricky dropped his popcorn and scrambled up and over into the arena. "Get the kids over the fence!" he screamed to parents and pick-up men as the bronc busted through. Panicked grandparents scrambled down bleachers, their arms reaching for little ones.

~ * ~

"Auntie, look!" Kay cried as she burst into the kitchen. Mona shut off the water, turning from the sink. "It's video…" Kay's breath caught as she thrust the phone at Mona, "…from Ricky's arena!"

Mona leaned down, focusing on the screen. Shaking her head, she turned away padding quickly down the hall.

"Auntie?" Kay's eyes were wide, urgent for an answer.

"Help me get ready…" Mona called back, "…you must take me to Ricky."

~ * ~

The old Ford pulled into the darkened main gate as the last horse trailer was pulling out. "Drive up to the bleachers," Mona said to her niece.

Kay leaned forward, looking side to side. "It's all roped off,

Auntie…I think we have to go back around…use the cowboy entrance to get that close."

"Okay…just go find him. I'll wait here."

Kay parked the pickup and stepped out.

"Roll down my window, Kay…stupid child-locks are on." Mona shook her head. "Seventy-six years old and I still can't open my own widow."

Kay chuckled, punching a button, "All yours now, Auntie."

Mona rolled down her window. The cooling air carried heady scents; sweet hay, fresh manure, the exhaust of a diesel tractor just shut down for the night, the fading waft of popcorn. She closed her eyes. It was a summary of her life.

Mona was born into horse tradition. Trussed to her mother as soon as she could hold her head up, she went along checking cows on horseback. At four she was riding her own pony alongside. She started competition rodeo as a teen and after many successful seasons took an offer to train horses. She still got an occasional call.

~ * ~

"Thanks for bringing her," Ricky's scarred fingers squeezed his cousin's shoulder. "I suppose what happened is all over the damn social media."

"At least no one got hurt."

Ricky breathed in deeply. "Yeah…I've wanted to believe it's…" Ricky's voice quieted, "…just in my head."

Kay nodded. "Trust your mom." She suddenly snorted, "Eee… you'd better put her to work…we had to dig in her closet for the ribbon shirt grandma made…I had to steam it to get the wrinkles out then drive her all the way here…I didn't do that for nothing."

Ricky chuckled. Turning, he spotted his mother step slowly around the bleachers. Taking hold of a post, she slipped the toe of her turquoise boot between the fence rungs.

"I thought you left her in the pickup?" He pointed to Mona with his chin.

Kay shook her head, chuckling. "She told me she couldn't walk that far."

Ricky hadn't studied his mother from afar for a long time. Her black jeans sagged, and her back was slightly stooped, but the turquoise silk of her blouse hung from her narrow shoulders in perfect symmetry. Ribbons of yellow and black rippled as she tossed back her long white hair. It was the same shirt she'd worn that night.

Some called Mona a horse whisperer. Ricky knew his mother had a deeper connection to horses than just being a good trainer. His boots sank deeply into the dirt as he crossed the arena. After dimming the lights, he crossed back, unlatched the main gate, and stepped out to her.

"I'm sorry I didn't…" he started to apologize.

"No." Mona hushed him. Her head was raised. She was an antenna, absorbing what could not be seen.

He scanned the bleachers behind her. They were empty except for Kay. Turning to his mother, he waited to speak. Finally, her head lowered, and she turned to him ready to listen. "How do we know he'll come back?" Ricky asked softly.

Raising a hand to his shoulder she patted him lightly. "The horse is our relative," she said nodding. "He is not our enemy." Her hand slid to his back, and she nudged him forward. When they were inside the arena she spoke again. "Can you see how he's been trying to communicate? His spirit needs honor and respect returned to him …it was taken from him in life."

Ricky had refused to believe her back then. He'd dismissed her words as the musings of an old mixed blood woman who'd been around horses so long, she was believing in legends. Since he'd been the manager, the arena had never had a close call like this. If it hadn't been for Riha, the grandma and the little girl wouldn't have made it over.

"I felt his spirit the night you rode him," his mother nodded to the first chute, "even from up in the stands. I could feel the heat of his eyes…all through his bucking, rearing…his fall."

"But…I didn't break his back, Mom!"

"No…you didn't…you are not to blame," she assured him. "You acted just as a cowboy should…just as you were trained to." Mona nodded. "This bronc didn't buck because he was born and bred to…he bucked because he'd been bullied. He was trained to hate his two-legged brothers, and this is what it has led to."

"But how…how did I see those same eyes, Mom…" Ricky shook his head, "…in the bronc last night?"

"I don't have that answer…I just know his spirit and yours too …are wounded and unsettled. This has to stop." Mona's voice was strong, and it was more than a simple statement; it was a proclamation.

"I don't want anyone to get hurt…the way he was coming for us…coming for me. After I went over the fence, he calmed right down…became a different horse."

Mona looked from her son's face to the moon above. She patted his arm. "It's time to tell his story…maybe that will release him… release you both."

Ricky stepped away from his mother as she steadied herself firmly. She began to sing almost inaudibly, like a fluttering flag. It grew to a rhythmic murmur and finally a strong melodic call. She'd trained horses in this way. She sang to them the soft chants she'd learned as a child. Doing so calmed them, gained their trust.

Ricky closed his eyes. His mother's singing drained him of anxiousness. His feet began to feel sturdy, as if he'd been planted, his roots spreading through the arena. He heard the dust first, felt it's fine spray against his cheek. Opening his eyes he could see the wind swirl it, like dancers in a circle. He crouched low as his mother's notes rose, higher, louder.

His thoughts fled as he was carried aloft into the swirling. Pulled into the sky he was spurring the bronc. Its nostrils flared with pain, and he saw the shift to anger in their descent. He felt the stab in his own haunches as rider became horse and horse, rider. He jolted up then spilled down from the stars. Just as he remembered how it felt when the bronc broke his fall; he would soon feel the crush of being broken.

The world turned upside down as the sky became earth. Hate was blood-shot yellow as his eyes rolled and his bones cracked. All became still but the tug as his body was pulled away through manure and dirt.

A hazy film blew away like frost. Ricky heard a distant whinny and faint retreating hooves. He sensed a dim light above him and stars further beyond. His mother's face appeared, then Kay's and he felt their pull until he stood on rubbery feet. He was no longer broken. As his awareness returned, he felt the shed of something. Relief washed over him.

~ * ~

It was Round-Up week again; Ricky was telling stories. There was a lull, and the group went quiet.

"So, Ricky." A cowgirl pushed back her hat, glanced around the circle of friends. "A guy told us a bronc nearly killed you…thirty-some years ago. He says that's why you quit riding. Is it true?"

"Yep." Ricky nodded slowly. "You probably wonder why I never told you that one." Ricky breathed in, then exhaled. "It's a long story to tell…took me a long time to know how to finish it." Ricky scanned their eyes, reading their confusion. "You're all lookin' at me like I'm crazy, now."

"Just tell us…even if it's long…even if it's crazy," the cowgirl urged. "We might not remember anything by morning, anyway."

Ricky chuckled.

It was later than usual when Ricky closed the main gate that night. A calm breeze once more carried the familiar sounds and smells of his livelihood. The young men and women had listened silently, soaked his words up like sponges. He'd told them exactly how it happened, how it took him years to get over it. "Whatever you want to call it, flashbacks, restless spirits, shapeshifters…that's up to you.

"It was a tragedy that twisted my gut…but working through it gave me a greater respect for the dignity of all living things. It gave me an appreciation of all the people I work with in this sport…and I mean even the ones you don't see, parking cars, cleaning toilets, popping the popcorn, signing your checks if you're lucky." A quite ripple of laughter spread through them.

"After I became manager, my mother convinced me to make visits to the stock contractor's facilities. I wasn't even sure what I was looking for. I could see the difference in the stock though. The ones humanely trained, treated with respect…they were full of life. The others…and I only saw a few…were mean, hateful, and broken.

"For years I thought I'd been robbed of my future. But now I realize that sometimes it takes a bad incident to shake things up for the better. You kids are part of a much safer, more humane sport now… It's taken hardship, but we've weeded the bad eggs out…at least in this arena." He smiled at their solemn faces. "Now…who's gonna give me a ride down to the Cove…you still buying Trevor?"

~ * ~ * ~

CL Prater grew up on the Rosebud Sioux Indian reservation of south-central South Dakota. A retired educator, she now lives with her husband on a busy little farm along a Nebraska river. She does chores, gardens, writes, babysits grandkids, and volunteers at her local rodeo's concession stand. She's published a variety of poetry and non-fiction; "The Release" marks her first published work of fiction.

TOUGH AS FAITH

Tisha Marie Reichle-Aguilera

Daddy took me to Brawley for a junior rodeo when I was in fourth grade. We sat next to another dad and his daughter Grace who was about my age, but shorter. She wore a shiny pink shirt, and her hair was in two tight braids like mine. But her braids had pink satin ribbon woven through them and pink plastic fairy barrettes decorated the top of each one. She had a denim skirt and white boots that would be dirty before the end of the rodeo, I was sure of that.

I wiped my sweaty hands on my jeans and stared at the scuffed toe of my almost too tight boots. Next year, maybe I could be in the arena instead of sitting here with the fans. Maybe these folks clapping and cheering for the ropers and bronc riders would be chanting my name when I win barrel racing or breakaway roping. I've been practicing every day.

Grace and her dad were there to watch her older sister, Faith. She was tall but not skinny and had her hair cut short. With her cowboy hat on, I thought she was a boy. That was probably part of her plan because Grace whispered to me Faith was competing in chute dogging. It was a boys-only event.

I had never seen chute dogging before, so I watched the first boy intently. He dragged the steer by its horns across the chalk line in the dirt and wrestled it to the ground in about twelve seconds. He made it look so easy. The second boy was taller and skinnier, came out the chute kind of hunched over and slow. He went to the ground before the steer and got a hoof in his crotch. The crowd erupted in an "Oh!" before the boy let go. That's a disqualification. The third boy was short and looked muscular in his tight denim shirt. He lifted his chin to someone in the audience to loosen his hat before getting in the chute. He grinned and smacked his gum. I don't know why he was so arrogant. That steer drug him out past the white line and kept running right out of his hands. Maybe he didn't wanna get dirty by twisting that snotty nose into his shirt and landing in the dirt. The fourth boy went way past the line but held on and eventually managed to wrestle his steer down. He got up with a poop stain on his back.

If the mothers in the audience knew Mr. Black let his daughter enter this event, encouraged it even, they'd probably be mad. I know my mom would have reached over the fence and snatched me by my trensa. She would have yelled at Daddy like she had done when I entered calf riding last year. Daddy reminded her the burns on my arm are from when I helped her in the kitchen, and I almost lost a finger when I chopped tomatoes with a dull knife. That calmed her for a bit. But she never stopped trying to get me interested in dancing like my cousin. Her efforts were futile. All I ever wanted to be was a cowgirl.

Most moms here have been preparing their teenage daughters for the Brawley Cattle Call Queen competition since they were younger than me and Grace. There are at least six of them standing around the announcer's booth with crowns on their cowboy hats and sashes that would definitely be in the way if they were riding or roping. The sun glinted off their giant belt buckles. I couldn't see their names engraved in the silver, but I knew it was there. Knew I wanted a big shiny buckle like that one day, but *not* for being a queen. I wanted one for barrel racing or breakaway roping.

Clearly, Faith didn't care about being royalty either. And I didn't see a mother around to offer advice.

That first boy was still in first place when the announcer called, "Faith Black, you're up." He had less enthusiasm than he had for the other contestants, and he didn't play a little bit of music while she was getting into place like he had for the boys. Did he know she was a girl?

Daddy and I joined Faith's dad and sister whistling and stomping our feet on the wooden bleachers. I yelled as loud as I could. I wanted Faith to know I wanted her to win.

Faith positioned herself next to the steer. Between the metal railings of the chute, we watched her bend her legs and brace her arms like the boys before her had done. Her steer let out a loud snort. Snot went everywhere. Including all over Faith, but she didn't loosen her grip. There was a loud bang of metal on metal and as the steer leapt out of the chute, Faith did too, as if they were one creature. As soon as she crossed the line, she planted her feet and turned the steer's head toward her. But the slippery surface slid out of one hand, so she wrapped that arm around its neck. That made it angry and it let out a loud noise. Faith was strong, but the angle was all wrong. The steer pulled its head up and then down as it half-growled, half-shrieked. Faith didn't let go. She used all her weight to wrestle it to the ground. It kept fighting after the timer stopped and its sharp horn ripped through Faith's black jeans. The steer got up, but Faith didn't. There was blood. There seemed to be a few seconds without sound, without movement, followed by an explosion of screaming, yelling and running.

Daddy tried to turn me and Grace away from the scene, but I peeked between his legs.

Mr. Black ran down the bleachers two at a time, a loud "No!" dragging out of his throat.

Within seconds, the paramedics were in the arena with a gurney and Mr. Black stretched his arms out, like Jesus on the cross, to move the crowd away from his injured daughter.

Grace scooted closer to me, her breath hot on my neck. She squeezed my elbow and whispered she would never be in a rodeo.

~ * ~

Faith came out of the hospital on crutches at about one in the morning. "Looks worse than it is," she said. "I'm starving."

We handed her the first-place belt buckle for chute dogging one of the queens had given Grace before we left the arena.

That day, I knew I wanted to be as tough as Faith.

~ * ~ * ~

Chicana Feminist and former Rodeo Queen, **Tisha Marie Reichle-Aguilera** (she/her) writes so the desert landscape of her childhood can be heard as loudly as the urban chaos of her adulthood. A former high school teacher, she earned an MFA at Antioch University Los Angeles and a PhD at the University of Southern California. Her fiction has been anthologized and nominated for awards. She is the author of the YA novel *Breaking Pattern* (Inlandia Books 2023) about a girl who loves horses more than people and the prose chapbook *Stories All Our Own* (Bottlecap Press 2024) about rebellious girls who defy gender expectations. She is a Macondista and works for literary equity through Women Who Submit. You can read her other stories and essays at http://tishareichle.com/

COUNTRY COUSIN

Gerri Leen

He's never been in a place so…close. Buildings taller than anything he's seen rise so high above him they block out the sun. The street's a line of shadows, and he feels cold and has to repress a shiver. It's winter, and he knows it's no colder than Cheyenne, but the New York City chill seems much more bitter than Wyoming's. He feels compressed by all the metal and concrete around him, the cold wind focused and seemingly aimed right at him.

He feels colder when he thinks of Diablo. Two more seconds on that bull and he'd have been in contention. His brother told him that considering it was his first time back since Thunderbolt had nearly killed him, he'd done great, but he knows he can do better and that's why he's out on these cold, gray streets, trying to walk off his frustration. He thought the fresh air would make him feel better, but the air's not fresh and he doesn't feel better.

In fact, he's never felt so alone before, even though there are people everywhere. Plus, he has no idea where Madison Square Garden is other than behind him…maybe. He's disoriented and there aren't any landmarks to help him get his bearings. Just endless rows of big buildings.

He thinks about asking the woman next to him for directions, but she's staring straight ahead, and then she walks before the little walk signal appears. So do others, hurrying to avoid cabs hurtling two abreast down a street that looks like it should hold only one.

The taxis are yellow missiles, barely guided. He rode in one yesterday from La Guardia—he wasn't sure he was going to survive the trip. The last time he was that scared was when he rode his first bull, back at the rodeo in Cheyenne. That was ten years ago, and nothing's ever come close to scaring him that way. Until now, in this big, big city everyone compares to an apple.

Have these folks ever seen an apple? Because it looks nothing like this. The big part he buys, though. He's never seen anything as enormous as this place. When he looks up, he feels dizzy. Earlier, in his hotel room, when he looked down, he felt dizzy, too. Is there a place in this city of honking and sirens and people where he won't feel that way?

He waits for the walk signal and feels the disdain of every person who pushes past him. They move like a school of fish, and he's the rock they have to get around. As long as he doesn't move, everything's fine. But the moment he's in motion, he disrupts the flow, not moving fast enough, not walking straight enough. He stops to look at something and gets bumped by a large man who calls him "Buddy" and then "Moron" when he still doesn't move.

He sees a spot of green up ahead and hurries toward it. The spot turns into trees and grass, and he realizes he's finally reached the park. When he asked the guy at the front desk of his hotel where the park was, the man had made it sound so close, maybe not factoring in that he walked six times slower than a New Yorker would. Maybe the guy's never seen a man amble down a street. He's looked and no one else seems to be taking their time. Not that he hasn't seen plenty of tourists. Because they're out there, all right. But they seem to be shrill and zipping here and there with their maps and cameras, and they all wear blindingly white sneakers. He avoids them the same way he would a skunk on the trail.

Hunching a bit into his jacket, he considers his cowboy hat, beat-up old boots and worn-in jeans, and knows he probably looks like an ad for cigarettes. If they still ran those ads, which they don't much anymore—the government being so concerned for its citizens' health and safety. If the feds are so damned concerned, they should do something for the safety of a pedestrian in Manhattan. Now that might be useful.

His brother's been on him to quit smoking. Funny, he doesn't lecture him to quit bull riding, and that's a lot more likely to end him. Almost did, when Thunderbolt turned on him at that event in Abilene. Damned bull got under his vest and gored him deep in the side. He felt it a split second before he realized what the hell was happening, then the bull rushed over him, his hooves breaking ribs his horns hadn't already taken care of.

It still hurts if he stretches wrong. It hurt today when he fell off Diablo. He imagines it might hurt till he dies. He doesn't know a bull rider who doesn't hurt somewhere.

He wanders the park and for a while forgets where he is. Except even here there are people everywhere. It's a pretty day, and he thinks the whole population of Wyoming could squeeze in here. Providing he took out a New Yorker for every one of his people. There is no such thing as big, open spaces here, that's for sure, but at least he doesn't feel all pressed in. He can finally feel the sun on his face—even if the wind is blowing cold and hard still—and something inside him settles down for a spell.

He's hungry but he doesn't want one of those hot dogs from the little carts. He's heard he shouldn't eat from those, that not all the vendors follow the health codes. He thinks about the times he's roasted a hunk of venison over a fire and wonders why he's suddenly worrying about health codes. But he heads out of the park and back into the land of shadows until he finds a deli, just clear of the business district, almost with the brick buildings his cab driver told him were residences when he asked about them.

He goes to the counter and orders a corned beef sandwich, because that sounds authentic New York to him. He has it on rye, even though he really likes white, and lets them fix it their way. He eyes the bottled water, but can't bring himself to pay that much for what ought to be free. Coke is familiar, and he grabs a can and a bag of chips and pays for his meal.

He could pay for a lot of meals in Cheyenne for what this sandwich is costing him. What this damn trip is costing him. Two more seconds might have made it all okay.

The sandwich tastes good, though. He's parched and hungry from his walk, so he finishes it and the Coke off in record time.

"Guess someone liked his sandwich," a soft voice says.

He looks up and sees a young woman, probably in her early twenties—though it's hard to tell here because all the girls seem to wear their makeup and clothes so sophisticated—and she's smiling down at him.

"First time in Manhattan?"

"That obvious, huh?" He knows it is. He hasn't seen anyone else who looks quite as rustic as he does.

"Well, we don't get a lot of Marlboro men around here."

"Bull rider."

"I figured. Saw the highlights on the news." She looks him over. "You win?"

"Not hardly."

"Well, you'll get 'em next time." She laughs and takes his tray.

"You want another Coke?"

He's still thirsty, and he starts to get up. She pushes him down, and he's startled, realizing it's the first contact he's had with someone here that doesn't involve jostling on the street.

"You sit. I'll get it." She's gone a sec and then back with a plastic bottle. "You can seal it up and put it in your pocket while you're sightseeing. Much more practical than a can, and won't freeze your hands off when you hold it."

"Thank you kindly." It's what his ma drilled into him to say, and the girl laughs. He reaches for his wallet, and she shakes her head.

"My treat. Consolation prize." Another cute grin.

"That's awful nice of you."

She cocks her head and studies him, like that little dog on those old commercials. "You think people here can't be nice, don't you?"

"Hasn't been my experience that they are." He leans in. "I bet you're not from around here."

"You'd lose that bet. I'm from two blocks down. My dad owns this deli. And his dad owned it before that. It's a family business."

He's never thought about there being family businesses here. Well, other than that really famous "family business" that the Italian folks run.

"You know what your problem is?" Her voice is still soft, so he thinks it might be safe to venture he's not sure what it is. "You're seeing New York as one big place. One big city with one big crowd of people."

"Well, yeah. That's what it is."

"No, it's not. You have to look for the individuals. You have to find the small things that make up the city. Did you know there are all kinds of neighborhoods in Manhattan? Places where people have lived for years and never moved, never wanted to leave because it's home."

"Yeah, well, that's all fine, but those places aren't real apparent to a guy like me. I'm stuck in the bigness."

She leans in, her eyes sparkling. "We've already established you're a betting man." She winks, and he colors a little. "I bet you a free dinner here—whatever you want—that you can find ten people to connect to if you start looking for individuals in the—"

"School of fish?"

"Yep."

"And I get a free meal if I don't?"

"Anything you want. But you have to try. Scout's honor, okay?"

"I wasn't a boy scout." Boy Scouts are for people who need to pretend they grew up in the woods and mountains.

"Whatever. Just say you'll try."

He gets up, tucking the bottle into his pocket. "I'll try." Then he smiles. "I think you're just betting I won't be able to find my way back here."

"You got a phone?"

He laughs. "Broke it."

"Of course you did." She walks him to the door and grabs a piece of paper off the counter, writing the address and the cross-street on it for him. "There, cowboy. No excuses." She winks at him again. "And you have to come back either way."

"I do?" He sounds a little surly in his surprise, and she reacts just like a girl would back home, looking down and turning a bit red. He tries again. "I mean, I will."

She smiles. "And if I win, you take me out to dinner over there." She points to a pizza place down the street.

"You're on, miss."

"It's Sarah."

"Sarah." He tucks the address into his pocket and leaves her with a tip of his hat.

As he walks, he quits looking up and starts looking at the faces in the crowd. He sees an old woman beaming, then she tries to hide her smile as she starts to cross the street.

He catches up with her. "Terrible cold day."

"Oh, it is." Her smile is out again.

"Is the cold a happy thing?"

She leans in. "I just found out I'm a grandmother. Little boy. Vincent Andrew."

"Just today?"

She nods. "I'm on my way to the hospital now." On some kind of impulse, she grabs his arm and squeezes. She's a little thing, and he barely feels the touch through his jacket, but it still means something.

"Congratulations, ma'am."

With another smile, she lets go of him and heads down a side street.

He walks on, studying the people he sees. A man who looks like he's lost his best friend. He sees a kid playing with the dog he's carrying rather than leading. He sees a tall woman who has blue hair. He sees…individuals, and it suddenly doesn't feel as cold here among the steel and concrete.

"Hey, Mister." It's the kid with the dog.

He turns and waits for him.

"Did I see you on TV today?"

"I doubt it, son."

The boy looks as if he's been struck.

"I say something wrong?"

"That's what my dad used to call me." The boy hugs the dog closer. "He left me and my mom, and he never comes to visit. She's working so I have to take Ranger out."

It's the kind of stream of consciousness talking even a kid in Cheyenne would probably do. He might even name his dog Ranger.

"I'm sorry. That's rough."

The boy studies him. "You ride bulls?"

"Yeah."

"Why?"

It's a hell of a good question. "Well, I guess I like it."

"That's weird. They can hurt you."

He doesn't say people you love can hurt you more. He has a feeling the boy already knows that. "Yeah, I guess it is weird."

"You want to walk Ranger with me?"

"I could do that." He sees a bank with an ATM. "I've just got to make a stop." He's gonna need some cash; he has a feeling dinner will be on him.

Country Cousin first appeared in
This Ain't No Rodeo – WolfSinger Publications – 2008
Reprinted by permission of the author

~ * ~ * ~

Gerri Leen lives in Northern Virginia and originally hails from Seattle. She's passionate about horse racing, tea, and collecting encaustic art and raku pottery. She has stories and poems in *The Magazine of Fantasy & Science Fiction, Nature, Strange Horizons, Dark Matter* and others, has just published her first poetry collection *Unwilling: Poems of Horror and Darkness,* and is a member of SFWA and HWA. See more at gerrileen.com.

HOW TO ROPE A BULL

Marri Champié

Courage is being scared to death…and saddling up anyway.
—John Wayne

I have a love hate relationship with cell phones—Droids actually —and with my Droid in particular. I love it because it's like the dope, science fiction thing, the Universe at my fingertips. I mean seriously, what's not to like about the whole "Okay, Cosmos, show me a picture of the shipwreck of the Tempest, lying at the bottom of the Mediterranean," thing, complete with instant pictures and videos? The payment is that I am now at the beck and call of the Cosmos. "Okay, Indy," (infer deep, echoing voice) "I have something I need you to do now." It always wants me when I'm in the middle of something. I guess that's what I wanted when I started writing Science Fiction, so I shouldn't complain. But it can't spell for shit, because it changes "shit" to "shot" and "fuck" to "duck" and its ridiculous autocorrect inserts something completely unrelated to what I intended—like "what do you do when the Taurus crashes?" when I clearly said "what do you do when a horse is cast?" —which somehow takes all the magic, science-fictioness, out of the whole process.

DroidBoy did the little "you-got-a-call-ring-ring-answer-the-damn-phone" ringtone thingie as I was loading my roping horse into the trailer one late Wednesday afternoon. We're talking Khasino now, the roping horse Morgan gave me, and he's as no-nonsense a horse as they come, so we paused with his front feet in the trailer and his back feet still on the ground while I answered the phone. I imagine he took a nap. I hoped it wasn't Morgan, canceling our roping date.

Cat's voice was breathless, like she was running. Her voice is a bit rough anyway, but this time she squeaked. I realized she was panicked.

"Indy!" She was an octave too high.

"Hey girlfriend. Why're ya breathin' hard? You doin chores, or is the gardener boy there?"

"Not funny. I need help. What are you doing?"

Sounded like she was going to cry. I have this fear inside about Cat, a premonition something bad is coming. She's beautiful and sad and poetic, like a lovely piece of old silver tarnished to an unrecognizable state of blackness but so exquisite underneath it takes your breath away at unexpected moments. Everyone she's loved has died. I mean, I can't even find a way to tell you her story—about her wild husband Tony who died to pay a debt to demons, about her son who died a war hero, about her famous designer mother who died disappointed. About her tormented sister who overdosed. About her baby brother who lived only a week with a faulty heart. About her last guy who left to be a trucker. About Danny-boy, who she expects to leave any moment. I can't tell her story, but her eyes do. And I'm afraid for her.

"Going to a Jackpot Roping event in Kuna with Morgan," I said. "What's up?"

"There's a big, red bull in the garden. He's got Danny pinned in the garden shed. Danny's hurt and he's pissed."

"Who? Danny or the bull?" I asked.

"The bull. He ate some of the Red Dirt and he's out of it and pissed off because Danny tried to get him out of the garden." Red Dirt was the cannabis of the season Cat had growing in her tomato plant row.

"I'm on my way," I said.

Morgan was just pulling into the parking lot of the roping arena when she answered my call.

"My friend, Cat, needs help with a bull that's rampaging in her garden. How set are you on this roping event?"

"Always ready to help a woman in distress," Morgan said.

"I'll be at the arena in a few minutes. Pull out and follow me."

We arrived at Cat's within fifteen minutes, parked, and assessed while we unloaded and saddled our horses.

Cat was right, it wasn't funny. Cat's horse, Navarre isn't a cow horse. He's big, he's black, and he's beautiful, but he isn't cowy. He's part Friesian. That's a euphemism for not-very-useful—sort of like English majors. The kind of horse knights rode back in the day, to pack around armor and swords and pikes and lances and shields and some fat-ass who had to look chivalrous while killing enemies. Cat looked...perched. And fabulously chivalrous, of course.

Friesians prance. Like in a parade. Like the horse in "Ladyhawke," complete with platter sized hooves, hair-feathered legs, and a mane and tail no one in their right mind would want to wash and comb. So, Navarre was pissed, prancing back and forth with his tail dragging vegetables around, and he obviously wanted Cat to run her pike through the damn bull. Cat nudged Navarre at the bull, to push him away from the shed. Navarre pranced up, faced the bull, pinned his ears, bobbed his nose up and down angrily, and grumbled. He reminded me of a picador's horse at a bull fight, minus the pica. In response, the bull snorted, jumped up from his camp at the shed door, pawed the dirt, shook that big head, and ran at Navarre, who promptly retreated. Then bull went back to the shed and laid back down. Round won.

We eased our horses up and staged beside Cat and Navarre. In this country, bigger is supposed to be better. So, that should've made Navarre better, and Cat a decorative ornament on the sovereign of the hill—or garden in this case. But that pig-eyed, overweight, red bull had staked his claim to Cat's garden, and no black-tie affair in a fancy horse suit was gonna pull down his territorial flag. Don't even try to tell me pot makes the user mellow, or that eating it is better. That big-ass bull was mad as a politician running for president, and intent on killing Danny-boy if he ever came out of the shed.

Morgan's roping horse, Orofino is the primo bull handler. She takes him to jackpot roping events instead of one of her younger horses because I'm her heeler, and I'm a ditz, and she knows we'll have a chance if she rides Fino. It's not Khasino's fault his rider—me —has all-thumbs on two left hands and sometimes ropes his head instead of the cow. With Morgan and Orofino on the business end of the cow, I have plenty of time to be inept and we can still turn in times no one can beat. We're a damn good team since three out of the four of us know what the hell we're doing; I just go along because two riders are required in team events, and Khasino can't roll the rope back up by himself.

Navarre pinned his ears at the bull and the bull didn't give a crap. Bull eyed us, the newcomers, and still didn't give a crap. Bull was king of the garden, and keeper of the shed. He shook his head and slobbered.

"Danny-boy," I yelled. "What the hell did you do to this bull to piss him off so bad?"

"Ohhhh, god, Indy, ...nuthin," he said. "Get me outta here."

His voice was thin with pain.

Bull had eaten an entire Red Dirt plant, Cat's cash crop. Apparently, pot doesn't bring out the pacific bovine nature, and he was gonna get even the moment Danny emerged from the big green box. Bull was standing guard, which at the moment was actually sitting. Like Ferdinand sitting in the flowers, but with his full bull mean on. Did Ferdinand eat daisies, or was it poppies? Can't remember.

That over-confident red roast must have figured if the biggest and blackest horse in the county would back down, he didn't have to worry about horses. He figured wrong. Morgan shook out her rope. That's one cowgirl right there I would not mess with if I were a bull —stoned or otherwise. Orofino lowered his golden head until he could stare Ferdinand right in his beady little eyes. I've heard stories about how Orofino handled the meanest bull to ever walk a ranch, so, if anyone had been there to take my money, I would have put it all on Morgan and Orofino right then. Ferdinand snorted and clambered to his feet.

He was the most humongous bull I'd ever seen. Not the sort of thing we roped at the arena on a Friday night. He was the Diplodocus of Bovines and doubtless weighed in at over a ton. A horse, even a cowhorse, is lucky to weigh half that. Fino is stout so maybe he came in at half-ton plus a couple pounds. Bull's eyes were red-rimmed and glazy, tiny in a head the size of the cooler we take salmon fishing. A half-dozen dewlaps obscured his stubby front legs, and he was humped like a camel above his shoulders, rippled with muscle and fat. Bull's horns were curved down around his face, and tipped with brass weights, which made him appear as though he was wearing a jester's hat. Weighting the horns is a safety feature on the full-size bovine models, so the rancher doesn't get poked. Trouble is, you can't easily rope a bull's weighted horns because the horn tips are tucked too close to the head for the rope to slide under. A bull's neck is probably the strongest part of him. If you have horns to wrap a rope around, you can lever his head back and swing him around. If you lay the rope around that muscle of a neck, you better have some serious poundage on the managerial end of that rope—like maybe a D10 Cat with Cooper Atwood at the stick.

Ferdinand the Red snorted and slobbered. He threw his head and sent strings of white mucus that splattered the side of the green shed and his red coat. I wondered how high a cow could get from eating a pot plant. I mean, don't they eat it twice? Like regurgitate it and chew it again? Is that a double whammy? I ruminated on this idea.

"What are you guys doing?" Danny asked. "Are you gonna get me out of here? Fucker broke my arm."

"Hold on, Danny-Boy, the Queen of cowgirls and her super-horse are going to handle this big bad dude," I shouted. "But you might wanta give her a minute or two."

Bull heard Danny's voice. Whatever Danny had done—most likely nothing, knowing Danny—that big hunk of meat was not gonna forget until someone turned him into steak. He got back on his feet, lowered his head, and rammed the shed. Wham.

"Hey," Danny shouted.

Wham Wham —Ferdinand hit it again with the side of his head where the horns protected his face. Some of the wood caved in.

"God damn mother..." Danny yelled.

Wham. Wham. Wham. Ferdinand tipped the shed off its brick foundation. Stuff clattered inside the shed. Danny was just yelling now, incoherently.

"Hey, garden-boy," Morgan shouted. "Shut the fuck up!" He did. Morgan is small, as women go, but her low voice sort of growls with a snap, so people just hep-to.

Morgan nudged Fino forward and gave the lasso in her right hand a little swing, easily looping it over the bull's head. Her hands blurred as she dallied that rope around the horn. Morgan turned Fino away and urged him into a lope to pull the bull away from the shed. She nodded at me over her shoulder. That was my cue to get a rope on Ferdinand's hind legs. I shook out my rope. Fino felt the weight hit the rope, and swapped ends to face the bull and keep the rope tight. Fino had his hind end down, dug in his hooves, and tried to back up, all his weight and force on that rope. That horse is a powerhouse when he's all bunched up and digging in like that.

I touched my leg to his side and Khasino moved in, aiming for the big red ass end. See that's what they all do for me, so I can just concentrate on my aim to get my loop over the back feet while Fino pulls the animal toward him. It's easy peasy. Usually.

Not this time. Ferdinand was having none of it. Fino might be the meanest, fastest, toughest roping horse on the planet but that bull was twice his weight, double stoned, and madder than twenty hornets whose paper nest was hit with a stick. Chuck Roast staggered maybe two steps, then braced against the rope. He eyed Orofino and Morgan, lowered his head, pawed the ground, and grunted. He staggered right, then left, as if he couldn't quite get his feet under him. Then he pawed the ground again.

"Awh oh," Morgan said. "Indy, hold off," she yelled.

Yeah, I'd figured that out already. The rope tightened downward when bull dropped his head and pulled against the weight on it, so the saddle on Orofino tipped forward and the rope dragged him down in the front end. Morgan didn't let the dally end go though. I told you she's fearless.

Ferdinand charged. He ran straight at Orofino, his head set just below shoulder height, his angry eyes clamped on the golden horse. It doesn't take more than a half a breath to run the length of a rope, when the rope is barely the length of three bulls the size of Ferdinand. But Orofino is fast. That horse leaped sideways as the rope slacked, whirled on his front feet, and let fly with both of his back feet. He caught Ferdinand on the side of the neck and head with a blow that sounded like a sandbag hitting a sidewalk after falling from the top of the Empire State Building. T-Bone staggered and tripped, his front legs buckled and his nose plowed dirt.

Morgan set Orofino to plunge away, and they dragged that red hunk of burger about twenty feet before the bull finally got his head up, and his feet under him to brace against the rope again. He stopped Fino in his hoofholes, and the horse's back feet went out from under him. The bull's weight pulled Fino down, so horse and rider went over sideways and backwards. The fall pinned Morgan's leg under Fino for a couple of seconds, before the horse righted himself and lunged to his feet.

You want to know the craziest thing about that moment? Morgan did not come off. And she was still aboard and in charge when Fino surged back to his feet. If that had been me, I would have been rolled up in the dirt, dead or wishing I was, waiting to be crushed by 2000+ pounds of flat iron steak. Not Morgan. When she's on a horse, she's hot-glued to the saddle. Hot being the operative word. Yep, she was hot all right. Mad as hell. And Orofino too. He'd had enough.

Orofino charged the bull from one side and hit him with his chest at about mach 2. Ferdinand rolled off his feet, went clean over, then Fino spun and pulled. The bull's head dragged and tons of dirt went in his eyes, so he couldn't see anything and probably wondered what the hell was happening when Orofino turned back, reared up and used his front feet to tenderize the bull's head. Orofino is a placid horse. I mean, babies who can barely sit up by themselves can ride him safely. He's like the Santa Claus of horses, big, easy-laughing, cookie-loving, friend to kids and dogs. He must be a Gemini, because this yellow demon horse I was looking at, pounding that bull's head into chicken fried steak, had to be Fino's evil twin. And Geminis always have an evil twin.

What were Cat and Navarre, and me and Khasino doing while all this was happening? Hmmmm. Well, besides leaping this way and that to stay out of the way, not too much that could be called useful. I mean, what could we do? There was the meanest, toughest cow handler-pair I knew, being dragged around by a monster, stoned, choice-grade, red bull. I thought more than once about trying to get a rope on Ferdinand's back feet, but somehow, that seemed like an extraordinarily bad idea. Now that the bull was dragged away, Cat placed her horse, Navarre between the bull and the shed, a testament to her fear for Danny-boy's safety. I was worried the bull would take that badly and target them.

I shook out a loop again. Why am I always in situations with Morgan where I feel like I need to take action, but I have no clue what action to take and feel helpless? And stupid. And scared. If I could get a rope on Ferdinand's head too, maybe together we could drag Stewie somewhere. Like out into the road to play.

Bull came to his feet once more and shook off the dirt. He was a mess, his eyes and mouth full of mud. He staggered, dazed, or stoned, I'm not sure which was working harder. But he was still angry. He bounced right, butting the air with his jester horns. Then he bounced left, snorting and slobbering. He turned around, and I realized he couldn't see. Morgan backed Orofino up slowly, to tighten the rope just enough to get Ferdinand to move and hopefully not resist. Fino's ears were pinned to his head and he looked like a golden dragon. His ferocious gaze was riveted on that bull. Cat was muttering behind me, speaking softly so as not to draw the beast's attention, urging Danny to stay put until the bull was subdued. Morgan moved him a dozen yards away from the door.

The rope stretched taut again. I nudged Khasino with my knees and he stepped forward, cautiously. His resistance vibrated between my knees. He's vegan, you know, and something of a pacifist as horses go. He didn't want to get involved in this blood-feud thing between Ferdinand and Orofino. I touched his withers with my gloved fingers to reassure him, and he relaxed, his head dropping a few inches.

"You can do this," I said, to myself, and to my horse. I was lying to myself, but Khasino believed me. He blew air out his nostrils with a rolling sound.

The sound of Khasino's snort caught the bull's attention and he swung around. The rope tightened. There was a row of stout pine trees beside the shed. Morgan backed Fino around the largest one so the rope was half wrapped around the trunk, giving her a fulcrum of leverage to hold the animal and get a bit of relief from the bull's direct weight. With my hands shaking almost uncontrollably, I swung the rope and looped it over bull's head, first try. It wasn't like he was a difficult target, after all he weighed a ton, and was about ten feet away, not moving. He'd be pretty hard to miss, actually, except I was shaking. I dallied the rope, scared. I knew we couldn't hold it. I kept my fingers outside the rope and locked the butt of my hand against the curve of the horn. Couldn't type those science fiction stories if I lost my fingers when the damn rope slipped.

I backed Khasino in the direction of Fino and Morgan, at about a ninety-degree angle to Morgan's rope so if he charged, we could both split apart and keep the bull between us. Trouble is, Khasino is not all that stout. Not like Fino anyway. He's half Arab, and any stout he got from his cowhorse mom was modified by his pretty-boy dad. What he lacks in body weight though, he makes up for in heart. When he felt the weight on the rope, he did what he's trained to do, he got his haunches down and put pressure on the rope to keep it tight.

Ferdinand didn't like it a bit. He started bucking and pulling. Beneath me, the heavy saddle shifted forward on Khasino's withers. My heart beat so hard it slammed in my ears, and the pulse in my throat was like an alien trying to break out. I had a death grip on the end of the dally, and it burned the leather of my gloves. I think I grunted. Or maybe that was Khasino. Then suddenly, Cat was there, in front of Ferdinand. Navarre stepped in close and stamped his feet, shaking his big black head and that crazy long black mane so he looked like a whirling dervish. The bull tried to charge him, but was restrained between Khasino and Fino by the two ropes. Cat turned and trotted Navarre in the direction of the barn and corrals. I backed Khasino in rhythm with Orofino and we made it about twenty yards and were out into the gravel of the big wide barnyard before the bag of red jerky woke up and decided he wouldn't cooperate. He began to buck and kick and whirl and grunt. He got his foot over my rope and as he twisted around, bucking, the rope wound round and around his front legs.

It was like reeling in a fishing line, only we weren't doing the reeling, Ferdinand was, and we were the catch.

"Can you hold him?" Morgan shouted.

"I don't know!" I screamed it, much to my embarrassment. "No," I wanted to say. But you don't say no to Morgan.

I tried. Ferdinand was wound so tight he could barely move. He sat down and eyed us balefully, breathing hard. I considered letting go, because we were dangerously close to the bull. But that would leave Morgan and Fino holding him all by themselves again, and out in the open now, with no trees for leverage. Bull had peed and crapped on himself, and he was covered in sweat. His rank stench made my stomach heave. Khasino trembled, but held like he was trained to do. He was no Orofino, and I almost thought he might break, or come unhinged, but he didn't. He was as steady as Fino, though a bit more scared, and a lot less mad I imagine. Nothing scares that big gold horse of Morgan's. Cat was trying to get the gate open to the round pen. The high corral sides of the pen would keep the bull in, certainly. I just couldn't figure out how we would get him in there without getting turned into spam, and then let Prime Rib loose and still get out before he tenderized us.

"Let's try to get him in the round pen," Morgan said. "I'll go first, and I'll get the rope around the hitching post in the center while you let the rope go and get out of the pen."

"What about you?"

"Don't worry about it," she said. "Just man the gate so I can get out without letting the bull out too. Can you do that?"

"Sure," I lied. I would barely be able to woman the gate.

"Oh, come on writer-girl, ya big sissy. You held a gun on a bad-ass drug runner, you can stand up to a bull."

Just to clarify. I held up the gun and had considered shooting about equally with the other option—running. In the end, Morgan's other half, Galien killed the drug-runner, and left me wishing I had closed my eyes for the whole fucking thing.

From my perspective, I could see how tight across Orofino's withers the rope was. The rope had even burned some of the hair from his neck, and white lather had formed a line along the rope's length against Fino's hide. Morgan had both fists on the dally end and wasn't even touching the bridle reins looped over the saddle horn.

A diesel truck and trailer rattled into the barnyard. The racket made Khasino flinch, and he moved sideways a few inches so he could turn his head to see. That gave the bull enough slack he was able to scramble to his feet, and stood there wobbling, his front legs connected to my saddle horn by a short length of very tight rope. He was breathing hard and white showed all around his bulging eyes. A white truck stopped beside us, and a cowboy jumped out. He wore a plaid shirt and had a ball cap on. Another guy got out of the passenger side, a taller guy in a white shirt and straw cowboy hat.

"Get the horses," the driver said to the man in the white shirt.

"What's the plan here, ladies?" the cowboy driver asked, removing his ball cap for a second, then replacing it firmly.

Cat jumped from Navarre and tied him to a ring on the hay barn post.

"Brand!" she said.

"I see you found Ole Red," Brand said.

"Yeah. In my garden. Danny tried to get him out and he trampled Danny. Broke Danny's arm. I have to get Danny out of the shed. This is my friend, Indy, on the black horse, and Morgan Gunn on the gold one. Have you got this? I need to get Danny."

"Go on. See to Danny. I'll help these ladies."

Cat ran toward the shed. Brand turned to me.

"Brand Little," he said, and touched the brim of his ball cap.

"India Alexander," I said. Don't know why I got so formal all of a sudden—must have been his touch-the-hat chivalry. I struggled to keep hold of the dally braced in my numb hands. "This red freezer full of burger belong to you?"

"He does indeed. Broke down the fence this morning. We've been hunting for him." He turned to Morgan. "Morgan Gunn? From Donnelly? I know your dad."

He touched his cap again, lifting it slightly. The other cowboy led two bay horses up beside Khasino.

"This here's my best hand, Shorty," he said, and took the reins from the tall cowboy. "Looks as though you had a little trouble," he said.

I snorted. Wasn't sure which was funnier, the lightpole of a cowboy's clichéd *"antoname,"* or that he made slight of our death duel with this pile of bull crap

"He tried to ram the shed where Danny's hiding. Knocked it clean off the foundation." Morgan said. "He's too big for my horse to hold, angry as he is. Took us a long time to get him here."

"Hey, can we just dispense with all this yakitty yak shit, and shoot this sucker?" I asked. The rope was slipping through my hands and my gloves smelled like they were burning. I was gonna lose my end of the rope in just seconds.

Old Ferdinand was getting his second wind, and as Brand swung his leg over that big bay horse, the red bull came back to life. He started bucking and pulling, snorting, and flinging mucus. He pulled Khasino to his knees and dragged us. The only reason he didn't come at us was because Orofino backed up and held that rope tight. Red grunted and bellowed. He fought with his massive head, flinging it back and forth, pulling poor Khasino along on his knees. I was afraid we were going all the way down. We crossed the gravel, Khasino squealing in pain.

Brand Little looped out a rope and noosed it over the bull's head. He dallied up and pulled that bull toward us, so Khasino could get up. Shorty swung his lasso a couple times and tried to heel the bull, but completely missed, the loop smacking against the back of Red's legs.

I didn't think about it. I couldn't hold on, and I wasn't letting that sonofabitch drag Khasino down again. I let go of the dally, and the rope burned off the horn so fast the leather smoked and left a burn mark on the horn. Out of the corner of my eye I saw Cat and Danny cross the gravel. He had one arm over Cat's shoulder, the other tucked against his chest, and hopped on one leg. He didn't look good. They were headed to Cat's truck, which was parked in the hay barn. I pulled loose the latigo on my back-up rope, swung it a couple times to get the loop big enough, and caught Red's two back feet, easy peasy. Just like a pro. Before I could pull it tight, Shorty jumped from his horse, grabbed that rope from my hands, and ran with it into the trailer. He passed it out the window.

"Grab this India," he said, "and take a dally. Try to keep just a little pressure on it. I'll get my rope on 'im too."

Shorty roped Red from the ground, got that second rope around Red's hind legs and ran it up through the window of the trailer. Morgan and Brand had Red fully checked from the front, so when Shorty got back on his horse, and took the end of his rope, he and I backed up the horses and dragged that bull backwards up the ramp into the trailer. The bull went in lying down and bawling in protest, his massive bulk a dead weight on the ropes, his sides heaving in exhaustion. The moment he cleared the back door, Brand jumped off his horse and closed the trailer door, pulling the two ropes off the bull's head.

Red got up, and stood somewhat quietly in the trailer, defeated for the moment. We slacked our lines and the hind ropes came loose. I pulled mine out and rolled it up, tying it back to the saddle. Red was swaying, bawling, and acting like he couldn't stand. He sat down.

Brand stepped up to the trailer and peered in at him.

"I don't think I can get that rope off his front legs until we run him out through the chute at the feedlot. I'll bring it back to you," he said.

"I'll just get a new one," I said. It probably stank.

"I have no idea what's wrong with him. He's usually pretty mellow." Brand jumped down from the trailer, shaking his head, perplexed. I wondered if we should tell him his bull was stoned. Ranchers probably don't go for the hippie bovine types.

Danny was seated on a hay bale, his back against the stack, and his eyes closed. If he hadn't been in so much pain, he would have been cracking ridiculous jokes about boobs and bulls. He was not grinning. Morgan had Danny's arm in her hands, feeling it carefully, and Danny was not even attempting to peer down her shirt.

Morgan is an almost-vet, you know, an extraordinarily beautiful one with extra nice boobs. Well, officially, she really is a vet now. Just a couple weeks ago, the U of I sent her degree. She'd only been missing credit for a single class when Rory was murdered, and she dropped out of the program forever. Her professor petitioned to give her the credits, and the University awarded her the doctorate. Her brother, Jordan, says she threw the certificate in a stack of magazines and newspapers beside the fireplace and didn't tell anyone. Jordan of course, rescued it, and hung it in her barn. So, she's now officially a DVM, and she can do stuff like look at Danny's arm.

"Broken," she said. "Here," she touched a place above the wrist, "the ulna, and here," she gently touched the humerus. "And the clavicle. I'll get some pain meds from my truck. Try not to move. I think he bruised your hip too. It doesn't feel broken but there's a hoofmark just here." She touched the spot and Danny yelled.

"That will be a big bruise. You need to go to the hospital. Those breaks have to be set. I could do it if we were up in Donnelly. I mean, I have all the stuff in the Vet barn to do that, but you need to see a real doc. This is your arm, it needs to be set right. The break on the ulna is clean, the break up here on the humerus, not as clean."

She came back with a bottle of water and pain pills.

"I don't have insurance," Danny said, worried.

"I do," Brand said. "Work comp will probably cover it, or my farm liability. Get your ass loaded up and in to the emergency room. Give them my number for the paperwork. I'll have my guys come over and fix the vinyl fence where he broke through it. And the shed. Damn bull anyway. Don't know what got into him. He seems drunk. Can't stay on his feet."

"He got yanked around a lot, and Orofino kicked the shit out of him," Cat said.

"That's a mighty nice cow horse you got there, Miss Gunn. I hope he didn't get hurt any."

"He's fine. Rope burn on his shoulder is all. He gave the bull quite a pounding, he was pretty pissed. You should check Red's head." She laughed at that. And winced.

"Whoa, cowgirl," I said. "You hurt?"

'Nah," she said. "Fino rolled on my leg when that shit for brains pulled us down. Just my knee. I'll be okay when I can walk it off. You need to see to Khasino. His knees are bleeding."

Cat and Brand helped Danny climb into Cat's truck and they left; she actually spun her tires in the gravel. I appraised Morgan. She was standing crooked, and leaning on her thigh.

"You don't look okay."

"Yeah, I'm cool," she said. "I'll be fine."

Me, I wasn't so brave. I was still sitting on Khasino. I didn't think I could get off, my knees were so shaky. Khasino had quit shaking. He was probably napping again.

"Nice catch, India Alexander," Brand said, patting my knee. "Not a bad heeler. You two compete together?"

"Just the small stuff," I said. "No one smart would blow any money on me for something big."

"No, you and that nice horse got some style. I'd go watch. Not too many horses can beat that palomino though, I bet. How's he in the chute?"

"Calm," Morgan said. "Never breaks a barrier, but he still comes out on time. That's where we were when Cat called, over at the arena getting ready to rope. I'm thinking we're done for today."

"I sure appreciate you two helping Cat with this. I have no idea what got into Ole Red. Look at him. He's sitting there, like...."

"Ferdinand," I said, "minus the daisies."

"I thought it was poppies," Brand mused.

"Well, let's just say Red ate himself a whole bouquet of mind-altering experience in the garden," I said. "And he must have liked it."

Brand Little tilted his head sideways, thought about that a moment, tilted his head the other way and raised an eyebrow.

"Well, I can't afford a bull his size with that kind of habit," he said real slow. "We might have to eat him."

He tipped his hat again and they loaded up the horses in the back of the trailer and left.

We put Navarre away, and made a pathetic attempt to get all the cherry tomatoes out of his tail. They were rather decorative, like some Beyer Christmas horse model. Who the hell would have a horse with that much tail to comb?

"I'm worried about Danny's arm," Morgan said.

"I'm worried about Cat," I said.

"Why?"

"I don't know. I have been having these premonitions, like somethin's gonna go way bad."

"You're such a candy-ass sometimes, Indy." Morgan grimaced when she laughed.

"Yeah, I am. Sweet little candy-ass me."

We took the bravest war horses anyone ever threw a leg over home to my house, doctored their wounds, and put them in the barn for the night with an extra portion of grain and an extra bale of shavings in each stall to up the sleep number on their beds. That also included more worried petting, and more kisses than my first date.

After that, we did something we hadn't done for a while—we got out the Glenlivet, poured two fingers, and drank it down in one swallow. Just like real cowboys. Then we drank more scotch, sat on the porch, and waited for coyotes to shoot at. Luckily for the coyotes, we were too smashed to see them. It took about a half bottle of Glenlivet, but I finally quit shaking.

~ * ~ * ~

Three-time Dell Award author, **Marri Champié** has often ridden horseback into The Sawtooth Wilderness. Pushcart nominated for poetry in 2015, she received the Boise State University President's Writing Award for fiction & poetry in 2013, an Oregon Poetry Association Award in 2018, & was Kingfisher Prize runner-up at Pulp Literature in 2024. Her novel, *Silverhorn*, released from Kasva Press in 2018; the sequel, *Firemoon*, comes out in the fall.

She works as a wildland fire support driver, and silversmith, and lives on a small ranch overlooking the Idaho Prairie.

Visit her website at: WriteIdahoWriter.com.

THE WILD COW SHOWDOWN

Terry Alexander

Randy Cobb licked his lips and stared down the line at the three other teams. He knew Sherwood King, the mugger for the second team. A big Cherokee, strong as could be. He had his nephews Jeremy and Chris do the holding and milking. They were going to be tough to beat. The third team had two big guys, and a blond-haired boy, but one of the men was running to gut. He figured that fella would get winded in a hurry. Ginger Wilson was on the last team. She was the milker, and her two uncles were going to hold the cow still for her to get the milk in the bottle.

"Randy, Randy, pay attention." Bob Andrews was our team leader. He had Big Jim Carpenter as the mugger. Jim was one of the strongest guys around. "When she comes out Jim plant your feet and slow her down. I'll grab her head and twist it."

He nodded and scanned the crowd. Everywhere he looked he saw people crowded in the uncomfortable hardwood bleachers of the rodeo arena. Randy knew his parents were out there somewhere watching him. He wanted to wave to them but didn't want to appear foolish to the other entrants.

"Put your fingers in her nose and pinch it hard, bite her ear too. Just as hard as you can." Jim nodded. "I'll work my way up the rope and grab her, between the two of us, we should hold her still enough for Randy to milk."

Bob rubbed his hands on his pants and watched the timekeeper. The man stood in a white circle near the chutes. At his signal, the gates would be opened, and all hell would break loose. The old fellah in the checked vest and white cowboy hat looked down the line.

"Is everybody ready?" he shouted.

"Let's go." Big Jim nodded.

The timekeeper got a positive response from the other muggers.

"Open the gates on the count of three." He licked his lips. "One, two…"

Randy glanced at the gate men. Each man stood poised by the

gate, the release rope in his hand, just waiting for the signal.

"Three," the timekeeper yelled.

The gates opened all at once, four angry, thousand-pound cows bounded into the arena. Confusion took over. A big black angus ran straight at the mugger for team three and plowed him down. He dropped the rope as the animal ran to the far end of the arena.

Randy's team drew a big black-white faced cow. She had a line of saliva hanging down from her mouth. She bellowed, dug her hooves into the earth and ran after the one that got away. Big Jim planted his feet in the loose dirt and held onto the rope. The cow muscled forward, dragging Jim. His boots plowed deep furrows into the dirt. Randy glanced over at the two remaining teams. Sherwood had planted his feet like Big Jim. His nephew had the red cow by one ear and was trying to get the other hand on the animal's nose.

Ginger Wilson and her uncles were doing good. One of her uncles had the rope wrapped around the cow's head and had managed to force her head to one side. The other uncle moved in and grabbed the nose, plunging his thumb and forefinger into the nostrils.

"Randy, come on boy, pay attention," Bob shouted. "Get ready." He ran down the rope and wrapped his arms around the cow's head. He bit down on her ear, stuck his fingers in her nose and planted his feet. Big Jim dropped to the back and caught the tail. He held it and the rope in his big hands. The cow kept fighting, planting her feet in the dirt, and leaping forward.

Dirt flew from the cloven hooves. Randy got a mouthful of dirt, as he closed in. He caught a glimpse of Sherwood and his nephews. The cow had kicked Jeremy, when he moved in to get the milk and sent the bottle spinning out of his hands. He had to run back and pick it up. That was going to slow their time.

He spit the dirt from his mouth and moved close to the cow's flank. She kicked out with her hind feet. Randy moved to the side and felt a little puff of air from the passing hoof. Bob planted his boots in the loose dirt. The cow's front hoof came down on his right foot.

"Oh hell." Bob spit the ear out of his mouth and screamed. The cow bounded forward and nearly shook him off. Big Jim reached out and pushed him forward, steadying him so he wouldn't fall.

Bob dug his finger and thumb into the cow's nostrils. He pinched down hard and gave her head a savage twist. He clamped down on the ear a second time and gnashed his teeth together. Big Jim twisted the free end of the rope around the animal's legs and twisted the line as tight as he could. "Get in there, kid. Get the milk."

Randy ran forward, the pop bottle in his left hand. He reached out and caught one of the cow's teats. The brute let loose a loud bellow and jumped up and down. He slipped the tip of the teat into the pop bottle, caught the upper part, and squeezed while he pulled down.

"Don't take all day. I can't hold her much longer." Bob screamed.

"I'm trying. I'm trying." Randy squeezed the teat herder. "She's holding the milk back."

"Keep your head and get the milk." Big Jim said. "We've got two other teams ahead of us."

Randy wanted to look around. He kept his head pressed against the cow's side and squeezed the teat. He felt it, a squirt came through the opening into the pop bottle. He did it again and was rewarded with another stream of warm white milk bouncing against the bottom of the pop bottle.

"I've got it. I've got the milk." Randy shouted, proud of his accomplishment. He glanced up to see Ginger break away from her cow, running toward the timekeeper. Jeremy had recovered and got milk in the pop bottle. He broke away from his team's cow and raced after Ginger.

Jeremy got tangled in the rope and went down. He managed to save the milk in the bottle, but his bad luck gave Randy an advantage. He chased after Ginger. He knew he was gaining on her. He heard heavy footsteps behind him and knew Jeremy was closing the distance fast. That knowledge gave Randy an extra burst of speed.

He drew even with Ginger. The timekeeper was just ahead. They both crossed into the circle at the same time. Jemery was a step behind. "Time, the man shouted. He reached out and took the bottle from their hands. "Ladies and Gentlemen, we have a draw." His voice rang through the loudspeakers.

"Both of you know there has to be milk in the bottle." The timekeeper held the bottles above his head. Randy nodded, he cut his eyes over to Ginger to see she was doing the same. He brought them both down and poured the contents on the ground. "We have a tie. Ladies and Gentlemen, we have a tie."

He looked at Randy and over to Ginger. "If both teams are

willing, we'll have you both back tomorrow night. One team against one team, with the promise of extra prize money for the winner. What do you say?"

Randy glanced over to Big Jim and Bob. Both men smiled and nodded. Randy licked his lips, tasting arena dirt. "We'll do it."

"We'll be here too," Ginger said.

"There you have it, Ladies and Gentlemen, be sure to come back tomorrow night for a showdown in Wild Cow Milking between these two teams." The timekeeper took a moment to build suspense. "Now let's finish the regular events."

Big Jim approached Randy and placed a hand on his shoulder. "Come on, kid. Let's get a burger and fries and enjoy the rest of the rodeo."

"What about a coke?" Randy asked.

"Sure, we'll get you a coke too." Bob grinned. "You know we have a chance for double prize money tomorrow."

"He didn't say double. The judge only said they'd sweeten the pot." Big Jim glanced over to Ginger and her two uncles. "They'll be back tomorrow too."

Randy cut his eyes to Ginger. He flashed her a wide smile and hoped he didn't look like an idiot. He wanted to talk to her, offer her a coke and hamburger, but his tongue remained still.

"Come on, kid. Let's Get that burger." Big Jim grabbed his shoulders and walked him from the rodeo arena.

~ * ~

Randy slept for a few minutes on the drive home. His father pulled to a stop in front of their house and killed the engine. He stood next to his mom while his father unlocked the front door. Thankfully, it was Friday, and he didn't have to worry about school. "Get a good night's sleep. We have to grind some feed tomorrow." His dad stood back and let the others enter.

He knew the routine, every Saturday they had to fire up the hammermill and grind feed for the calves. The yearlings always did well with the special blend dad concocted. He marched up the stairs to his room. "Night Everyone." He disappeared inside his room.

He stripped off his outer clothes and crawled between the sheets. Tomorrow looked to be a busy day.

~ * ~

His father's rough hand shaking his shoulder woke him early the next morning. He got up and got into his working clothes and went downstairs for breakfast.

His mother placed a plate with eggs and bacon in front of him. "Better eat up. Today is going to be a busy day."

"I figure we can be finished by three this afternoon, that'll give you three hours to get cleaned up and get to the rodeo grounds." His father sipped at his coffee.

"That's great." Randy bit the end off a slice of crunchy bacon. "I know Ginger and her uncles will be tough to beat."

"Don't worry, Big Jim can hold that cow steady. Just be sure to get milk in the bottle." His dad attacked his eggs.

"My brother got his team disqualified when he didn't get any milk in the bottle." His mom smiled at the memory. "They were mad at Charley for weeks."

His father slurped down the last of his coffee and polished off his eggs and bacon. "Come on. We need to do the chores before we start grinding the feed."

Randy finished his breakfast and followed his father outside. Together they walked to the barn. They had fifty young calves, fresh off the mama cows, waiting for feed. Randy filled the buckets with the corn and grass mix and dumped it out into the metal feed troughs. His father waited near the gate and opened it when Randy gave him a wave. The calves ran through the gate, running to the troughs and devouring the feed.

"I've got the molasses out by the hammermill. I'll get the corn and the hay ready." His dad disappeared out the back door. Randy heard the loud belch of a tractor's engine starting followed by a muffled roar. He walked through the side door to the hammermill.

Grinding feed wasn't an easy task. The idea was to put in hay and corn, stalks, and all, along with a touch of molasses and let the hammermill grind it into small bits. The items were placed on a small conveyor and taken into the heart of the hammermill, where everything was ground and mixed together. Randy lifted a bundle of cornstalks from the large trailer and dropped it on the conveyor and waited for his father to show up with the hay. His father arrived shortly with a trailer load of hay.

He backed the trailer close to the hammermill and climbed down from the tractor. His father grabbed a pair of plyers and cut the wire from the first bale and tossed half of it on the conveyor. He hit the button and started the hay and cornstalks moving toward the first row of teeth. Randy doused everything with molasses before it went inside. The mix was ground into small bite sized bits, air pressure drove the cut feed down a small pipe that dumped the mixture into a large fifty-gallon drum. They had worked for three hours and had filled several drums with the feed mixture.

"Let the belt clear and we'll take a break," his father said. "Take a few minutes and eat a bologna sandwich."

"Sounds good to me." Randy nodded. "My breakfast wore off a while ago."

His father killed the hammermill when the contents of the belt cleared the grinding teeth, and the bits went into the barrel. "We're going to finish early today." His father patted his shoulder as they turned toward the house.

They passed through the gate going toward the house and a yearling bull fell into step behind them. It got a running start, then ran straight at Randy, letting loose a bellow just before it butted him in the butt and ran away.

The force of the impact threw Randy into the air. He fell hard to the ground. "Are you all right?" His father helped him to his feet.

"Yeah, I'm fine." Randy grabbed his father's hand and let himself be pulled to his feet. A pain radiated in his lower back. Randy took a step forward and felt a sharp pain in his legs. He took another step and winced badly as his weight came down on his left leg.

"That's doesn't look good." His dad helped him to the gate and up the pathway to the house. Randy hopped up the steps to the front porch and hopped inside.

"What happened?" His mother moved a cushion from the sofa. Randy managed to hop to the sofa and drop into the cushions.

"That hardheaded calf got him." His dad removed his boots and placed his feet on the cushions. We need to call Bob and Big Jim, maybe they can get another milker for tonight's event."

"No, don't do that. I can make it." Randy leaned forward.

"Yeah, you really look like you could wrestle a grown cow tonight." His mom shook her head.

"I'm not going to wrestle her. Big Jim and Bob are going to do that. I'm going to milk her and run to the judge." Randy licked his lips. "I just need to rest a little bit."

"Alright." His dad nodded. "We're nearly finished grinding the feed. Get some rest and we'll see how you feel before the rodeo."

"Okay. I think I'll be fine." Randy limped toward his room.

"If you're still limping you won't be milking any wild cows tonight." His mom said as he turned into the hallway toward his room.

~ * ~

Randy licked his lips anxiously. The event was about to start. He rubbed a sweaty hand on his pants leg, thinking about the story he told his mom about his leg feeling fine. He'd taken great pains to keep from limping when she was watching. He hoped when the time came, he could run, and at least try to win.

"Are you sure you're up to this? Mike told me about the calf running you over." Bob glanced at the gate and the black cow inside. He shifted his gaze to Big Jim. "That cow was in the event last night."

"Yeah," Randy said. "She ran over the mugger last night." He looked at Big Jim. "Keep an eye on her, if she runs straight for you, move to the side and flick the rope around her feet."

"That might work." Jim nodded. "Bob, when I get her steady, you jump on her head and hang on."

"Don't worry about me, I know what to do." Bob glanced at the judge entering his circle. "Time to get ready."

"Ladies and Gentlemen." The announcer's voice squawked through the speakers. "I appreciate you all coming out tonight to attend the second night of the Gap Prairie Annual Rodeo. We have some of the finest cowboys in six counties competing tonight for the prize money." He paused for a moment. "Speaking of competing, last night we had a tie in the wild cow milking contest. So, tonight, the two teams who tied are going to compete against each other for double prize money."

Applause and cheers came from the crowd. Randy glanced at the section where his mom and dad sat. He thought for a moment he had located his dad. He turned his gaze back to Ginger and her uncles. They looked ready to take on the world and win. A sliver of doubt entered his mind. He pushed it aside, determined that win or lose he would do his very best in the event.

"At the count of three the bucking chutes will open, and the cows will be released into the ring." The announcer went silent for a few moments, building suspense. "The teams consist of a mugger who holds the rope, the holder, and the milker. When the milker has milk in the bottle he will run to the judge in the circle and the one who has the best time wins."

Randy wiped his sweaty palms on his jeans and licked his lips.

"One." The announcers' voice echoed through the loudspeaker. It seemed like the entire audience had gone silent.

He glanced over at Big Jim and Bob. The big man nodded. "We've got this."

"Two." Randy felt a flutter in his stomach. He glanced over at Ginger and her uncles. They looked ready.

"Three." The announcers' voice echoed. The gate opened and the cow jumped out, pawing at the dirt. The noise from the audience was deafening. The black cow ran straight for Big Jim. The big man darted to one side and flicked the rope. The lasso circled the animal's left front leg.

Big Jim planted his feet in the dirt and ran the rope around his waist. The cow stumbled ahead on three legs. Bob jumped on her head. His fingers sank into her nose, and he squeezed. He got his teeth on her ear and bit down.

Randy ran forward, He jammed the pop bottle up on the tip of her udder, grabbed her teat and squeezed. Nothing came out at first. Randy gritted his teeth and squeezed harder. He heard the roar of the crowd and wondered how Ginger and her team were faring. He pushed the impulse to get a quick look aside and squeezed the teat again. Milk came from the opening. The cow shifted her weight and the bottle moved away from the opening and he sprayed his hand.

"Come on, Randy. I can't hold her much longer," Big Jim shouted.

He repositioned the pop bottle and squeezed three times in rapid succession. The bottle felt warm to his touch, Randy broke away from the cow and ran toward the judge standing in his circle. Only then did he risk a glance at Ginger and her uncles. She was still bent down at the cow's udders.

Randy heard a renewed roar from the crowd, as he raced toward the judge. Pain ran from his knee to his thigh, he gritted his teeth and kept going. His injured leg went numb, he couldn't feel his foot and fell to the ground. His mouth opened on impact and his mouth filled with loose dirt, but he kept the bottle up off the ground and didn't spill the milk. He glanced at the bottle and knew he had it nearly half full.

From the crowd's reaction, he knew Ginger had finished her milking and was closing in on him. Randy pushed himself to his feet and ran awkwardly toward the judge, his gait was like a half jump with his good leg and a small step with his hurt leg. He sensed Ginger was right behind him. The judge stood in his circle, watching them race toward him with wide eyes.

The man held out both hands, Randy managed to get his bottle into the judge's hand half a second ahead of Ginger. A loud cheer came up from the audience. The judge looked at both bottles. They both contained milk. He emptied both bottles on the ground.

He stepped forward and raised Randy's hand. "Ladies and Gentlemen, give a round of applause to the team of Bob Andrews, Big Jim Carpenter, and Randy Cobb. The winners of the wild cow milking event."

The applause filled the arena. Ginger approached Randy. "Congratulations." She nodded. "How's the leg? Did you hurt it very badly?"

"No. It'll be okay." Randy licked his lips. "Can I buy you a pop or something?"

"I'm hungry. How about a burger from the concession stand." She smiled.

"Sure, I can do that. Just help me get out of the arena."

She slid under his outstretched arm and helped him toward the main gate.

"Hey, Randy, come on, let's go get the prize money," Bob shouted.

"Come on, Bob. We'll give him his money later." Big Jim grabbed his arm and tugged him toward the gate.

Terry Alexander and his wife Phyllis live on a small farm near Porum, Oklahoma. They have three children, thirteen grandchildren, and nine great grandchildren with one on the way. Terry is a member of the Oklahoma Writers Federation, Ozark Writers League, Oklahoma Science fiction Writers, Western fictioneers, and Tahlequah Writers.

Terry has been published in various anthologies from Airship

27, Pro Se Productions, Oghma Creative Media, Wicked Shadow Press, and Pen-L Publishing to name a few.

TOMATO SOUP FOR THE COWBOY SOUL

Sierra Forsberg

To be a rodeo cowboy is to dedicate your life to being a misunderstood American icon living in modern times. The lifestyle is simple, yet unfathomable for someone who only catches a glimpse of it from the lens of a weekend grandstand seat. It is a multitude of hypocrisies: loud, but quiet; steady and swift; cutting-edge, yet old-fashioned. Some of your best memories are the worst moments. Country music, Hollywood recreations, and U.S. history books are all mimicries of the sport. Rodeo is the backbone of American agriculture and professional sports, steeped in tradition and raw competition. To be a cowboy is to embody the person everyone wants to be, but no one truly understands, and yet it is a role that is deeply ingrained in all of us. The cowboy life is a paradox, blending rugged independence with unwavering community spirit.

How else do you explain the drive to compete in a sport that is 50% living up to tradition and 50% trying to perform better than anyone who has ever run in your event? Sometimes the lifestyle makes you feel like you are crazy, other times you've long accepted that you are. Is it the adrenaline rush? The demand for precision? Strength. Speed. Strategy. Many would say it is all of the above.

It's a sport that requires a commitment to constant scrutiny. Criticism comes from a judge and from your competitors. You face it from spectators, both the ones rooting for you and against you. Rodeo contestants endure not just the physical demands of their sport but also the emotional strain of public scrutiny.

It can look like being an old man and staying in the arena long after the young guns go home. It is a blend of rigorous routines and unyielding dedication. A heightened level of preparation is essential because the margin for error is razor-thin. Every second counts, and every move must be executed with precision and confidence.

It's a lifetime of ignoring injuries that would sideline most athletes because the show must go on.

And that's what some people might see it as, after all—a show.

A modern-day Barnum and Bailey that rolls up and rolls out with a string of acts in the middle. A chaotic display of rough-and-tumble activities. Each performance is a dance between man and beast.

The greatest show on earth.

Even with the kindness of calling it that, to experience it as a competitor is to know it is still so much greater. This spectacle is a living, breathing narrative of passion and sacrifice, a story written in the dust of the arena and etched in the hearts of those who live it.

No one would know better than a man who has lived and loved it.

If that man happens to be your grandpa and there's a lifetime of stories between the two of you, he probably still has one more to tell you. One more story to make you better understand what the life is really like.

He would say, "You can't truly appreciate the essence of this life-style from the outside looking in. It's only by living it day in and day out that you begin to understand its true nature.

"It's about the moment you settle in the seat of your saddle and your eyes land on the bridge between your horse's ears before you set off to ride.

"It's about falling into your normal routine even on the days your own body fights you to get out of bed, but the horses still need to be fed.

"It's about being tired. Really tired. Most of your hard work is started before the rest of the world is awake, and finished long after others have gone to sleep.

"How could anyone understand the exhaustion of driving twenty straight hours only to get to your destination and that is when your real job starts.

"At the edge of the arena you can hear the crowd, and you swear you feel generations of competitors thrumming in your veins. Behind the scenes, people are buzzing from the overflow of energy in the stands. The butterflies surge when you hear your name echo through the speakers and there is nothing like performing under the lights.

"Then the work itself comes down to mere moments. You make your run, but you break the barrier, and you're done for the night.

"Maybe you catch and the crowd goes wild, but your horse is young and spooks, dragging the calf as well as your hopes and dreams with it.

"You live the role of a rambler sleeping on other people's couches and calling four walls and a set of wheels 'home'. Some of the days are so cold you rely on a fire from a metal barrel, retired outside the arena, to warm you up in time for your run. Other days are a blur of activity until you're back in your truck heading to the next one.

"But some days are unforgettable.

"Probably because it's not often you forget your boots and your hat on the way to the same rodeo, but it's pretty nerve-racking to show up to check in wearing a ball cap and sneakers while you're still trying to figure out where you're going to find the rest of your western attire before the performance in an hour.

"If my wife was there, she would have never let me live it down if I had to turn out because '*honestly what kind of cowboy forgets his hat?*'

"I was embarrassed going from trailer to trailer asking for a bum pair of boots and avoiding the arena. You tell yourself '*Everyone has been there before*' but why did it have to be you?

"I figured my luck must have been switching up when I made a new friend who was a size smaller but still willing to lend his boots and hat after riding his horse in the earlier rough stock event. A man is never picky in a time like that, even at the risk of my hat falling off.

"If we're being honest, I don't think I could tell you how my run went that night. All I know is I was well past ready to turn in for the evening and it was still almost a hundred degrees when I got back to my trailer. My mind was reeling about how I should probably leave an extra pair of boots in here for next time when I went to turn on the generator and all I got was the ringing click of the starter.

"That's the other thing about rodeo. You're always hot. Really hot. Especially if you're going hard in the summer. You're away from home, uncomfortable, and at the end of the day you would do anything for a nice shower and a little AC.

"But on a night like that, when the cards just keep stacking against you, the echoes of doubt flood your mind and before long the only thing you're thinking about is going back home and hanging your hat up for good.

"Ah, that's right—I believe I either missed my calf or had been out of the money, but it was just another rough night in a particularly harsh summer. As I stood next to my trailer trying to get my generator to kick on, the guy who loaned me the boots walked by and asked if I had eaten yet."

"I hadn't—I had just enough money to fill my fuel tank home and, in my optimism, hadn't anticipated another night without a check.

"A run of bad luck has to end at some point, right?

"Instead, he invited me to join him for a meal and my stomach answered for me.

"He gave me a lift to a twenty-four-hour diner he knew was nearby and at that time of night it was just the two of us, side by side at the counter. When the waitress came over, I sat there quietly as he ordered a meal big enough to feed two men.

"Then he added on at the end '*and Miss would you mind bringing us a little bowl with just hot water and also some of those little soup crackers*'. He looked over at me and said, '*I'm going to show you a meal that's going to change your life.*'"

"We made quiet conversation as we waited. Both of us talked about the rodeos we'd been to and the ones we were going to go to someday. He didn't have any flowery words of advice, just the subtle reminder that ones like us had ambitions and my earlier frustrations seemed to slip away.

"It wasn't too long until the waitress was back with two cups of coffee and a bowl of hot water, along with the rest of the food and a few packets of soup crackers on the side. Before I could dig in, he grabbed a nearby bottle of ketchup and globbed a healthy lump of it right in the middle of the hot water. He crushed the crackers into the bowl, adding a sprinkle of salt and pepper. After placing a spoon in as a final touch, he slid the concoction in front of me.

"He declared it '*tomato soup*'. The only other explanation he offered was that I would never go hungry again, and he dug into the plates of food while I stirred the mixture and took hesitant bites.

"He was right. I never spent another trip on the road where I was forced to go to bed with a growling stomach. There would be plenty of nights where I wouldn't be in a position to afford steak and lobster, let alone a plate of bacon and eggs. But he'd given me the perfect solution for when I was short on money and in need of a quick meal.

"That summer had been filled with bad days, but I wouldn't categorize that particular night among them. I'd finished with a serving of warm food and some company. I'd been able to lean on another competitor to help me out and even though I'd forgotten my hat and boots, I never forgot the recipe I learned.

"Now I won't say it was a recipe that turned my life or career around, but it did change my mentality.

"How many people get the chance to live out their dream the way we do? And for someone like me to do it for as long as I have? I've competed twice as long as most athletes, and against men half my age. But to do so takes sacrifice.

"You sacrifice long days of travel and a good night's rest. It's the sacrifice you make when you leave your wife at home to chase a dream you both believe in, knowing that it's just more time passing where you will be away from your family. Yet, if you're lucky, the very thing that takes you away from home is also the inspiration for creating core memories with your kids and a skillset you pass along to them. It molds you and makes you who you are.

"It's a heritage that is passed down from father to daughter, and carried on through the generations. A select few athletes get to compete side by side with their families, and yet rodeo revolves around the legacies we create and the fierce yet friendly rivalries that exist.

"I have seen breakups between team roping partners that are more heart-wrenching than their divorces. The very best parts of rodeoing are the people. Whether they're your friends that you see at each destination or the old man who offers you a memorable meal."

~ * ~

Swapping old stories is enough to make anyone feel romantic when it comes to the things you feel passionate about. So much of rodeo is the moments that can't be put into words easily.

And yet most of the unforgettable days are because rodeo is also a romantic tragedy. The story is always heartbreaking and beautiful. Success is never guaranteed and for the most part you may be doomed to fail, but the beauty comes in experiencing what it means to live in the full range of human emotions. That is what the people on the outside can't understand.

When a check doesn't come, how else can you continue if you're not just a bit romantic about it?

You have to be in love with the quiet moments when you can reflect on how far you've come and where you're going next. Crave the loud moments that echo in your soul long after they've passed.

Cultivate the habits that keep you coming back day after day when your horse relies on you and your kids look up to you.

Navigating the highs and lows requires the same determination and tenacity as a committed relationship. It's a legacy of 'almosts' and a reputation built off tall tales. There is an element of longevity that can only be survived by commitment and a deep burning desire to stay within the sport.

Every successful ride or event is a testament to the hours dedicated to practice. Competitors must be athletes and vigilant caretakers, constantly striving to demonstrate that their love for the sport and their animals go hand in hand. It is a relationship built on mutual respect and understanding one another. To be a rodeo competitor and part of the culture is to be molded and changed. The struggles instill a sense of discipline and work ethic. Rodeo teaches resilience, adaptability, and perseverance.

The community becomes a lifelong network. Whether it's sharing tips on improving performance, lending a helping hand with equipment, or simply offering words of encouragement, the sense of camaraderie is palpable. The bonds formed are deep and enduring.

Beyond the surface, we all bear witness to the dedication and compassion that defines the true spirit of rodeo.

There is no single word that better captures the essence of a life spent in rodeo than romance. It means loving the sport with unwavering passion every single day. It's about seeing rodeo as both an adventure and a ballad intertwined, a journey filled with highs and lows, thrills and spills. The greatest romance of all is looking back on your life and still feeling that deep affection for something that has held your heart for so many years. To cherish those memories and experiences, and to know the love for rodeo remains as strong as ever, is truly unparalleled.

There is a joy in rodeo that lies in the journey. The experiences, the triumphs and failures, and the growth along the way create a rich tapestry of memories and stories that shape who we are as competitors and as a community. At the end of every day is a solitary prayer that you get to continue to experience more of them. Rodeo is a way of life, a testament to our heritage, and a celebration of the spirit that drives us all.

~ * ~ * ~

Sierra Forsberg is a first-generation horsewoman who married into a family of multigenerational rodeo talent and has been fortunate to share their legacy in all mediums, from social media to movie production. She is passionate about storytelling and aspires to turn her thoughts into timeless tales. In the meantime, she's been a content creator in the communications and marketing field for over eight years.

This story would not be possible without her husband and the cowboys who raised him.

More Great Anthologies from WolfSinger Publications

The Dragon's Hoard 3 – edited by Carol Hightshoe

In this anthology, twenty-six authors weave enchanting stories of dragons—from the fierce and fire-breathing to the wise and benevolent. Enter a treasure trove of tales where dragons reign supreme and hoards are more than mere gold.

Discover hidden gems of wisdom and magic within these lairs. Feast on tales that shimmer with magic, adventure, and the timeless allure of dragons. Explore the myriad treasures dragons hold dear and the legends that surround them.

From heartwarming tales of friendship and loyalty to thrilling adventures filled with danger and magic, these tales offer something for every dragon lover. Whether they are guardians of treasure, seekers of knowledge, or forces of nature: the dragons in this collection will ignite your imagination.

The Dragon's Hoard 2 – edited by Carol Hightshoe

Welcome to realms where dragons reign, treasures abound, and every adventure leads to magic. Explore stories that spark the imagination and might just awaken the dragon within. Are you brave enough to face the dragon and claim your prize?

From the unyielding grip of ancient magics to the cunning of those who seek dragons, their treasure or both—each story weaves a rich tapestry of magic and lore.

Whether it's a battle for survival, the forging of an unlikely alliance, or a humorous twist on hoarding habits, our authors invite you to delve into realms where dragons not only hoard gold but also secrets, spells, and sometimes, even friendships. After all, in the world of dragons, not all treasures are silver and gold—some are stories waiting to be told.

Borne in the Blood — edited by Carol Hightshoe

Delve into the mysterious and powerful world of blood in "Borne in the Blood"

This collection of enthralling stories explores the multifaceted essence of blood—as a symbol of life, a medium of magic, and a bond of kinship. From the chilling tale of a minstrel haunted by a spectral king to the whimsical account of a vampire ice cream vendor, each story weaves a unique narrative around the theme of blood. Encounter a woman whose body bizarrely intertwines with metallic elements and follow a girl's journey as she confronts her isolation due to her heritage. Feel chills as those who were wronged reach across the years to have their final revenge on the blood descendants of those who oppressed them.

Shifters, Vampires, Witches, and other ordinary and extraordinary folk—all bound together by that which they carry in their blood.

These tales will transport you through a spectrum of emotions, from the depths of fear to the heights of fantasy, as you unravel the mysteries and power that lie within the blood.

Proceeds from sales of Borne in the Blood will be donated to the Multiple Myeloma Research Foundation – themmrf.org/

Space Brides — edited by Dana Bell

Tired of those lonely dark nights? No one in your settlement suitable? We are here to help! We will help you find the bride or husband to keep you company, raise your children, and be your partner building a dream together. Contact us directly and give us your specifications. Success guaranteed.

In this collection of 15 testimonials read about the challenges and triumphs of some of our clients as they found love on the frontier of space.

From aliens to vampires, we brought these couples together and together they found acceptance and love—each in their own way.

A man with three kids finds an unexpected match in the brother of the woman he had contracted to marry when she runs away.

A woman running away from an abusive marriage finds acceptance and respect with a colony group that marries everyone to everyone in order to ensure they know they belong to a family.

A woman constantly rejected because of her skin color and origins finds acceptance and love with a wounded soldier.

Even though we encourage absolute honesty in your profile and correspondence with your potential spouse—many people don't. However, like some of the testimonials you'll read here; they still manage to expand their horizons—together.

Contact or walk into any of our offices 24/7. We are here to help you find that special someone and start a new future!

Other conditions apply.
Please ask for more information before contract is drawn up and signed.

The Dragon's Hoard — edited by Carol Hightshoe

Dragons are well known for their hoards—but not all hoards are created equal.

A young dragon starts his hoard with some very precious gifts.
One dragon shares her complaints about taxes with a friend as they wait for a lunch delivery.
Another dragon defends her most precious treasures against a group of greedy goblins.
And yet another may hold the solution to saving the Earth after a devastating apocalypse in his collection of bottled treasures.

In addition to the normal gold, silver and jewels here you will find dragons who collect many different treasures. 25 storytellers invite you to enter The Dragon's Hoard and share the treasures within.

Tails From the Front Lines 2 — edited by Carol Hightshoe

Come meet some of the four-legged members of Law Enforcement who also serve and protect.

Here our authors will introduce you to the brave K9 officers who serve alongside their human partners. They are their eyes, ears, noses and sometimes when necessary they are their shield, protecting others.

Proceeds from this anthology will be donated to the El Paso County (Colorado) Sheriff's Office K9 program in memory of K9 Jinx who was killed in the line of duty on April 11, 2022.

Ring of Fire – edited by Dana Bell

Enter the Ring of Fire, as unpredictable as the land masses shaking a city and volcanoes erupting covering the landscape. Could there be other reasons for these events? Or could these rings be more than a geological location.

> They may be dragons playing tricks
> or magic portals opened to mysterious realms
> or sacrificing the best work of a lifetime.
> Perhaps a rescue during a forest fire
> or an attempt to raise the dead
> or even while attending a high school reunion.

Journeys are taken to far off lands, another world, and through caves, each with their own unique twist.

Each tale presents a new idea on what the Ring of Fire could be. It is more than what many have been led to believe. Pull up a chair and warm yourself by our fires—just don't let yourself get burned.

Out of the Darkness – edited by Carol Hightshoe

Mental Health issues have long been stigmatized, with those facing them pushed into the shadows, often unable to deal with the darkness they find themselves trapped in.

In this collection, stories explore many types of darkness—Suicidal Ideation, Death from Suicide, Survivor's Guilt, PTSD, Chronic Pain, Chronic Illness, Depression, Death of a Loved One, Secrets, Bullying, and other forms of darkness are explored. Some related to mental health issues and some not, but all of them offer very human perspectives. As in real life, some stories have happy endings and sadly others don't.

We offer these stories of darkness without judgement, but with hope and compassion. Some roads should never have to be traveled —but we understand that for many they are being traveled alone.

Proceeds from sales of Out of the Darkness will be donated to the American Foundation for Suicide Prevention—for more information on AFSP please visit their website at: afsp.org.

For those who may be in crisis—PLEASE call or text 988 to connect directly to the 988 Suicide and Crisis Lifeline. For those outside the US please connect with your local lifeline

Never Cheat a Witch – edited by Carol Hightshoe

Magical curses. Arcane revenge. Being transformed into a frog. Things evil witches do to mere mortals who cross their path. But, what if there is more to the story...

Deals made with a witch are magically binding and can bring dire consequences to those who even think about breaking them.

Whether they are seeking revenge for wrongs done to them, helping others or simply trying to live their lives—it is NEVER wise to try and cheat a witch.

Open your spell book and join our authors as they relate tales of witches and mortals. From classic fantasy witches to modern day witches and even the legendary Baba Yaga. Good and Evil as well as every shade of gray in between. And, yes—there is a prince who is turned into a frog.

Time Capsules – edited by Carol Hightshoe

Time Capsules–history and mystery–a gift or a message from the past to the future. Messages that can easily be misunderstood.

What were the reasons for passing along a pair of pink, fuzzy handcuffs?

A glass vial containing a perfect dandelion puff?

A Japanese Katana?

A red and blue scarf?

A wooden spoon?

What magic do these items contain? What stories do they tell?

From the past to the future. Mysteries and meanings abound within these pages, as well as reminders of the things people find precious. What will you find?

US/THEM – edited by Carol Hightshoe

Fear of the *Other* breeds hatred of the *Other*

They aren't like us—so they must be bad...inferior... dangerous...

Humans are by nature social animals, but we tend to bond with other humans with whom we have something in common: beliefs, experiences, likes and dislikes, etc.

With the expansion of humans across the planet, it seems that, even as our numbers grow, we find ways to whittle our groups into ever narrower, specialized, and exclusive blocks. We target the *Other* for the most minor differences and interpret everything from *THEM* as an insult or an attack.

Within these pages you will witness hatred, intolerance and fanaticism as well as love, understanding and acceptance. Most of all, I, and the authors, hope you discover stories that will cause you to pause and think before condemning someone as being *THEM* and not *US*.

Crunchy with Ketchup – edited by Carol Hightshoe

It has been said that one should never meddle in the affairs of dragons—for you are crunchy and taste good with ketchup.

Come enter the dragon's lair.

Take your chances with other would-be heroes and heroines who decide to face off against one of the biggest, baddest predators ever.

Witness a dragon civil war.

Hear the true story of the Battle of New Orleans.

Find out what it's like in the belly of a dragon.

Discover why cats can spell disaster when stealing a dragon's egg.

Meet a group of dragon riders who protect us from nuclear devastation.

Follow legends of modern dragons, only to find something very unexpected.

And more…

Crunchy with Chocolate – edited by Carol Hightshoe

It has been said that one should never meddle in the affairs of dragons—for you are crunchy and taste good with chocolate.

Come enter the dragon's lair and roll the dice. Within these pages you will still meet some of the biggest, baddest predators ever—but if you are lucky, you will also discover some that have a sweeter side.

Meet a dragon with a soft spot for hard luck cases and another who is a hopeless romantic.

Enjoy a musical battle between a dragon and the specter of one of the greatest guitarists to ever play.

Meet a dragon in trouble with other magical creatures because he enjoys hanging out with human children.

Join a mother and daughter and their teams of dragons on a dangerous cross-country race.

Reconnect with an imaginary friend—who is not so imaginary and escape the isolation of the pandemic.

And more…

So enter in BUT tread carefully—remember you are crunchy and taste good with chocolate.

Visit us at wolfsingerpubs.com

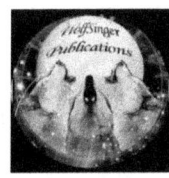

www.ingramcontent.com/pod-product-compliance
Lightning Source LLC
Chambersburg PA
CBHW071525170626
46811CB00007B/2957